The Deer King

The Deer King: Novella One

Ben Spencer

KNOCK-KNEE
BOOKS

ISBN-13: 9781732038004 (Paperback)

KNOCK-KNEE BOOKS

About the Author

Ben Spencer lives in Concord, NC, with his wife and daughter. Please visit benspencerwrites.com and sign up to follow his blog for information on new THE DEER KING releases. You can also follow Ben on Twitter at @RBenSpen.

For Charlotte

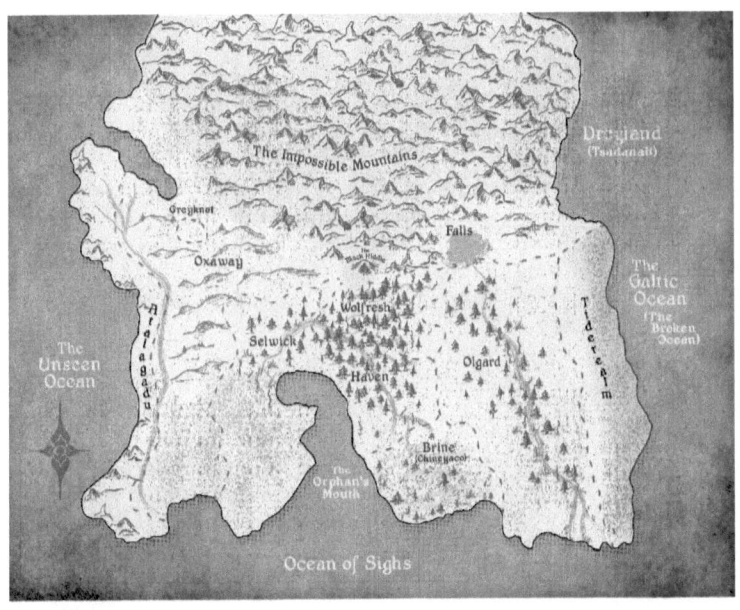

1

Brutus Rain was a man made of jagged bits and the blackest night, a man with old-world blood coursing through new-world veins, a man with a soul so gnarled that he didn't mind doing the dirty business of murdering prophecies in their cribs before they came to heinous fruition. But to Emmaline Rain, he was simply dad. In the small of the evenings, Brutus would chase Emmaline and her brother, Joseph, around the yard until laughter and exhaustion felled them, and then Brutus would gobble the children up in his arms, the kindest monster in the entire world. Emmaline especially loved her father's prickly kisses when the game was lost, the pleasant sting of them on her cheek. They were proof of her own strength, a girl so deeply loved by a man so deeply feared.

Emmaline was uncertain of her father's occupation. He wasn't like the other fathers in Mossbane (a city in the territory of Haven), the farmers and the blacksmiths and the store clerks and the soldiers, with their days full of routine and labor. She might have thought him a ne'er-do-well, but unlike the idlers who inspired scorn when they shuffled through the city streets, Brutus commanded an uneasy respect: he was never haggled with, or taken to task for a viewpoint, or questioned for his lack of participation in the culture writ large; furthermore, he was afforded an unrestricted line of credit in all the shops, and, if he ever needed a favor, volunteers by the bushel leapt to help, although the disquiet on their faces made it clear they did so out of an unspoken obligation, and not because they held a deep affection for the man. Emmaline might have worried about her father's strange station in the culture, but he was a self-possessed man, unconcerned with the perceptions of the others, and he passed these traits on to his children. Emmaline learned, over time, to hold her head high in Mossbane, and she soon found that people afforded her a respect akin to the type they showed her father.

This isn't to say that Brutus didn't have a job; only that Emmaline didn't know, specifically, what it was. She did know, however, that it was related to those times when a change would come on the wind, and Brutus, with no-nonsense speed, would hustle Emmaline and Joseph to their neighbors, the Houghtons, and then depart, usually for no more than four or five nights, although sometimes it was longer. His leavings had no rhyme or reason to them: he left in all seasons, and at all hours of the day. He once woke the children at three a.m. in the pouring rain, and made them tromp the quarter mile to the Houghtons' house in the mud and the muck. Emmaline, who was ten years old at the time, was certain that the Houghtons would at last object to being called upon at such an inconsiderate hour in such miserable conditions, but they only accepted the children as they always did, with prim good humor, and changed Emmaline and Joseph into dry stockings before ushering them to bed. Neither did his leavings occur at regular intervals. There were periods when he left multiple times over the span of a month, but there was also a stretch when he didn't depart for close to a year. Emmaline often considered asking her father why he left, but when the words rose to her lips, a terrible dread would course through her body, and she would think better of it. At last she gave up on asking him, supposing that he would tell her and her brother when the timing was right. Or perhaps, better yet, he would never tell them.

In the winter of Emmaline's thirteenth year—and Joseph's fifteenth—Brutus started pulling Joseph aside at random times and talking to him in hushed tones. Emmaline did her best to eavesdrop on their conversations, but her father, a vigilant observer of his surroundings even when relaxed, was careful that she didn't hear. She soon noticed, however, that her father wasn't merely conversing with Joseph; he was showing him something as well. On a number of occasions she happened upon the two of them looking at a small object in Brutus's palm, but the instant Brutus saw her, he would hide it away.

She asked Joseph to reveal what their father was sharing with him, but, on this matter and this matter alone, her normally loquacious brother went mum. "Tell me, Joseph," she pleaded, but each time she asked her brother, he would draw up his corn-silk moustache and purse his mouth shut. It frightened her, this uncharacteristic rigidness, for as long as they had been brother and sister he never hesitated to share his thoughts with her, even when discretion was called for. But on this subject he remained solemn, and mute.

At last, it happened. It was early spring, the fangs of winter not yet receded, when, on a brisk and windy evening with the clouds churning overhead, Brutus stirred to action. Summoning Joseph, Brutus proclaimed that it was time. Emmaline, who only moments before had been busy churning butter with her brother, watched with unease as the two men went inside to discuss the matter further, and, she assumed, study the secret object. When they returned, she knew what was coming.

"Let's go," her father said. "I'm taking you to the Houghtons'. Joseph is going with me."

They walked to the Houghtons' in a portentous silence, the burden of the great undone deed hanging heavy over the two men. Father especially seemed troubled: Emmaline sensed a seed of doubt in his bearing, and she wondered if it wasn't over Joseph and his preparedness for the task at hand. Regardless, they soon reached the Houghtons', where the men left Emmaline with unceremonious haste. She watched from the window of the Houghtons' ivy-strewn cabin as her father and brother departed, heading north by northwest in the direction of the kingdom of Wolfresh.

That evening she ate rabbit stew with the Houghtons, a delicious, garlicky meal accented with bay leaf and thyme. Later on, by the fire, Regina Houghton attempted to distract Emmaline from her worries by singing time-tested songs, some of which were nearly as old as the time of the first Harrish settlers. Initially the songs had their intended mollifying effect, but then the lyrics of one of the songs snagged in Emmaline's brain like a fishhook, and wouldn't let go. Emmaline waited until Regina had finished the standard—a paradoxically melancholic and upbeat tune called *Best Be Over*—and then she asked the question that had sprung to her mind.

"That line...*and if antlers sprout, don't go messing about, just summon the rain, it best be over*...what exactly does it mean? I've heard teenagers in town whistle that tune when they see my father. Is the song about my father? Is he the rain? Am I?"

Regina smiled. It was a forbearing smile, meant to hold time while she wrapped her head around a suitable reply. Emmaline had noticed this tendency in adults, a simultaneous desire to share the secret truth of Emmaline's life with her while keeping the selfsame fact concealed at all costs, like the way that Regina had sung *Best Be Over* on purpose but would now go to great lengths to conceal its meaning.

Dillon Houghton, the man of the house, stopped whittling the pinewood in his hand and stepped outside into the gloaming. It was clear that whatever was about to be said, he didn't want to hear it.

"That song," Regina said once her husband was gone, "is about how, when a thing goes awry, it's best to deal with it right away rather than allow it to grow into something terrible. It mentions the rain because the rain offers fresh beginnings each time it passes through."

Emmaline wouldn't be put off so easily. "But is it about my father?"

"I wouldn't know, child." Regina stood up from the rocking chair, dusted herself off, and followed her husband outside into the dusk. "No," she said as she left. "I wouldn't know at all."

That night, Emmaline dreamed about a boy, a tiny slip of a creature that stole into her family's cabin through an open window and begged Emmaline to hide him from a nebulous, unnamed threat. Emmaline agreed, but at once the boy's demeanor changed and he began to frolic about, tromping mud from his bare feet all over the oak-wood flooring. There was something mad about the boy's comportment, inhuman even, and Emmaline began to fret that she had made a terrible mistake, one that couldn't be undone. She tried to calm the child, but he only became more feral, galloping about the house with such spirit that it seemed he had entered a deep trance, and couldn't be reached. At last, Emmaline screamed at the boy to stop. To her surprise, he did, halting mid-gallop and pinning her with striated, green eyes. He asked, "Why? Is it time for you to kill me?" Then she woke up.

She looked out the window. It was morning, but outside, a grey peal of weather ruled, the roiling clouds from the previous evening having whipped into a boisterous storm. First it rained, and then it hailed, and then it rained some more, the precipitation coming in bursts, as if the sky were strafing the ground with grapeshot. The Houghtons, who were farmers, stayed inside and cast worried looks at one another. They spoke of the crops as if they were the concern, but Emmaline knew they hadn't planted any yet, so that couldn't be it. Finally Mr. Houghton, who had been pacing since daybreak, burst out of the cabin into the squall with a fevered and resolute look on his face, as if he meant to talk down the storm himself. But as soon as he stepped outside he came to a stop. Emmaline, who had a vantage point from behind him, saw why.

Walking down the dirt road from the direction of the kingdom of Wolfresh was Emmaline's father. He wore a suit of mud and blood, and there was a deranged look in his eye, like he was a man who had lost his soul and feared he would never find it again. Emmaline searched frantically for Joseph, but her brother was nowhere to be seen.

As her father drew closer, he caught sight of Emmaline. Seeing her, he fell to his knees and wept. The merciless rain beat at him without remorse.

2

One month later, a strange man arrived in Mossbane wearing the vestments of a priest of the Bronze Titan. The town buzzed upon the priest's arrival: word was that he had traveled all the way from Olgard's capital city to strip Brutus Rain of his station. Emmaline, who had been venturing into Mossbane on her own since her brother's death, learned of the priest's arrival in the farmers' market. She was there to buy fruit, but when she heard the apple picker speak her father's name, she knelt behind an apple cart and pricked her ears.

"Have you seen that mountain of a priest?" the apple picker asked the skinny man with the scraggly goatee considering his produce. "Bet you bottom dollar he's here to reclaim Brutus's stone."

"By force?"

"If need be. Brutus is a right big 'un; that's why they sent a monster. But make no mistake—they won't allow Brutus to keep his job, or the stone."

"It's true, then? That Brutus failed his last time out?"

"Priest wouldn't be here otherwise. Odds are there's a newborn Deer King suckling on its Massaporan mother's teat right now. A Deer King destined to kill a great many of us. And all because Brutus couldn't complete the one task he's charged to finish!"

"I'm not defending the man, but Titan's tits, Jonas, he did lose his son in the effort."

"Risk of the profession, aint it?"

"I suppose. What do you think will happen to Brutus once the priest is done with him?"

"He'll move east. He'll have to. There's no place for a man like that out here once his knife's gone dull. And good riddance, too. I, for one, don't want to look at him or his skulking daughter's face another day…"

And with those words Emmaline slipped away, swiping an apple as she left.

When she returned home, she found her father sitting on his bed in the corner of the cabin, turning a small object over and over in his hands and chanting under his breath. He didn't notice Emmaline for some time. When at last he saw her he gave a start, juddering like a mortally wounded animal. Upon seeing Emmaline, he started to put the object away, then changed his mind. He held up a blue-grey stone. As he did, a dirty tear slid down his face.

"Come here," he said in a weary, heartbroken voice. It was only the fourth or fifth time he had spoken to her in the past month. "Might as well take a look."

She drew close, trying not to seem overeager. "What is it?" she asked. She knew but she didn't know, the way children often have partial knowledge of the secrets the world of adults keeps from them.

"There are only two of these in existence in all of Dreyland," her father said. "The Effanarem call it a Funatan stone, after their Rain God, Funato. The Massaporans call it a Doido pebble, named for the Massaporan priest who stole the stones and gave them to our people. Most of the people in Haven call it the Saving Stone, but I call it naught. Always thought it best not to name magic. Thought not acknowledging it protected us somehow. I was wrong, of course."

"What does it do?"

He looked at her with distant-planet eyes. "You already know, don't you?"

Of course she knew. She had simply never admitted it to herself. "It tells you when a Deer King is born. And then you go and kill it. Only you failed to kill the last one. A Massaporan killed Joseph instead."

Brutus nodded.

They sat together in silence for a moment. She felt turned inside-out, the snakeskin of her childhood shed at last. She wondered if this was what Joseph had felt like when their father was teaching him the tricks of the trade. Sickly alive. Adult. She wondered if adults walked around with a pit in their stomach at all times, nauseous from the terrible knowledge of the world.

"Will you give the stone back to the priest?"

Brutus didn't answer. Instead, he turned the stone over and over in his hands, muttering a strange, foreign word, something that sounded like *Dachahelu.* As Emmaline watched, the image of a baby boy flashed mercury-quick on the stone's surface, and the stone seemed to pull, like a horse at the reins, in a northwesterly direction. Brutus stopped turning the stone, and the stone stopped moving.

"Your mother left when they made me a Stoneman," Brutus said, finding his voice. "'Choose', she said. So I chose. She left for Olgard the next day without saying goodbye.

"Most men wouldn't have taken the job, but I had seen what the last Deer King did to our people when I was a boy, and if someone had to bear the responsibility for making sure it never happened again, I thought it might as well be me. Taking the job was the only way I could make sure that the job was done right."

He sighed. "What happened…a month ago…was beyond me. Beyond anyone. No one could have stopped it. Simple as that. But it doesn't matter now. What matters now is that I right what went wrong. And I can't do that without the stone."

Emmaline was digesting this when she heard a horse whinny outside. She looked out the window and saw a colossus of a man sitting astride a magnificent Rugarder stallion, its red coat like brilliant roasting coals. Together, the man and the horse blotted out a good portion of the horizon. The man wore the black and white vestments of a priest of the Bronze Titan, and a pair of calfskin riding boots that must have cost a great many calves their lives. The closer the horse cantered to the cabin, the more surreal the man seemed. He had a beard like a black, roiling river, and mythic, monstrous eyes. He looked like the coming of death itself. He was the only man Emmaline had ever seen larger than her father, and he scared her out of her wits.

"Daddy, I don't think…"

"Go out back, Emmaline. Stay outside until he's gone."

She hurried out the back door but she didn't stay there. Instead, she climbed a ladder onto the cabin's roof, crept to the ridge, and lay down, staying as flat as a cat stalking its prey. Peeking over the top, she watched the priest dismount from the horse like a god stepping down from the clouds. She felt that he was staring her in the eye as he walked inside, but it was merely an illusion caused by his height. He hadn't seen her at all.

Once the priest was inside, Emmaline listened for sounds of conversation from inside the cabin. Words trickled out like water from a weak stream. Emmaline held her breath, trying to hear, but the sounds were muted and garbled. It was like attempting to eavesdrop on someone's dream. She gave up after a bit and prayed to the Bronze Titan, something she had never done before. She asked him over and over again to send his terrible servant away.

She was in the middle of her prayer when, out of the quiet, a great commotion kicked off, the sound of warring giants. Emmaline listened in horror. A half-minute later the racket subsided, like an avalanche coming to rest. Tears boiled in

Emmaline's eyes, hot and salty. She knew in her heart that her father was dead.

Without thinking, she stood up and walked over to the stone chimney. She dislodged the largest slab of stone she could carry from near the chimney's top, where a number of the stones had grown loose over time. Then she shuffled to the edge of the roof, balancing above the front door. She waited until she saw the top of the priest's head, his thunderous black hair like a storm cloud. A guttural, woeful sound escaped from her lips. Hearing her, the priest turned his face toward the sky. Emmaline dropped the stone. When the stone smashed into the priest's face, it made a sound like the cracking of ten thousand eggshells.

She hurried down the ladder and dashed to the front of the house, where the priest lay blocking the front door. His hands, she noticed, were slick with blood, and a spray of red colored his vestments. She knelt down and patted the priest's robes, searching for the stone. Tears and snot streamed off her. She knew that inside the cabin her father lay dead, and though she understood that there was no bringing him back, she thought that possessing the stone might open a door for her, one where she would find her father and brother on the other side.

Her fumbling hands grazed the handle of a knife inside its sheath. Stunned, she jerked her hands away. But only for a moment. Resuming her search, she felt a hardness near the priest's right ribcage. She slipped her hand under the vestment and discovered a hidden pocket. The stone was inside. She grabbed it.

The instant the stone was safe in her hand, the priest stirred. His extremities slowly dredged the air, sifting for consciousness. Emmaline stood up and backed away, watching him closely as she went. The priest's caved-in face was a swirl of dark colors. One of his eyes was closed over like a tomb. His other eye was half-open but it was impossible to tell if it was fully functioning. A black bolt of thought encouraged her to pick up the stone and smash it on his face once more, but while she was indulging the notion, the priest's good eye expanded to three-quarters and locked on hers.

She ran.

3

She was halfway to the Houghtons' when she changed her mind. She needed to flee Mossbane entirely. Heeding her instincts, she rushed into the forest, heading north toward the creek that marked the boundary of her previous woodland excursions. Her father had always warned her never to go farther than the creek, the reason being that the Wolfresh border was that way, and beyond the creek he couldn't guarantee her safety. But at the present moment nothing seemed more dangerous to Emmaline than remaining in Mossbane.

She made the creek in ten minutes, then continued running for thirty more. She had heard her father comment that the Wolfresh border was farther away some days than others, but most of the time three miles did the trick. She had always assumed that what he meant was that after three miles you might run into a Massaporan. When at last she stopped running and started walking, it felt to Emmaline as though she was halfway to the Impossible Mountains, but the thought of the priest trailing her spurred her onward, toward exhaustion.

Half an hour more and she collapsed against the trunk of an oak tree. Generally speaking, she knew how to orient herself in the woods, but she had ran too far with the wolf of fear nipping at her heels, and now she was lost. She would have cried, but her grief was too heavy; she thought that if she sat long enough against the tree trunk she might simply sink into the ground, and there be buried. Her thoughts were a black swarm of bees, her head gravity's slave. Together, they took her under.

She awoke to a pitter-patter of voices. A boy and a girl—both four or five years younger than Emmaline—were sitting on their haunches no more than five feet away, bouncing tinny words off each other in heavily accented Harrish, staring their fill. Emmaline's first thought was that they were Massaporans, but upon closer inspection she wasn't sure: their skin color was creamier and their bodies squattier than the few Massaporans she had seen. Also, they were speaking Emmaline's language, albeit in a clipped and high-pitched brogue.

Noticing that she was awake, the girl looked over her shoulder and called out "Ded!" Seconds later, a short dumpling of a man appeared from behind a copse of trees. His body was shaped so that it appeared he was contesting his kids' respective claims to paramount compactness, and his skin was a dull, greyish white, which contrasted unflatteringly with his retreating red hair. He waddled toward his children in apparent good humor. To Emmaline's surprise, his good humor didn't disappear when he saw her, although his lips did form an astonished O.

"What have we 'ere?" he asked as he drew closer, his curious eyes like brass coins. Over his shoulder Emmaline saw another figure step out from behind the copse of trees. A Massaporan woman, through and through.

"She's a girl, Ded," said the boy.

The man chuckled. "She is, isn't she?" the man said, dropping to his haunches like his kids. He had the thighs of a prize bull. "Havenese, from the looks of it. You're too far north, dear," he addressed Emmaline, his voice honeyed with kindness. "You'd best go home."

His words were a suggestion, not a command. Emmaline was frightened, but she summoned the courage to speak nevertheless.

"My family is dead. And the others don't want me there." She omitted mentioning the priest, though he was foremost in her mind; she imagined him standing guard at the border of Haven like an avenging angel.

The man didn't reply, only continued studying her, weighing his thoughts. In the meantime, the woman made her way up the hill. When she approached, the man turned to the woman and they shared a look that was both a question and an answer. The woman didn't exude kindness the way the man did, but neither did she look cruel. She simply seemed wary.

"We're travelers," the man said, "heading home. We live northeast, in the country of Falls, in the place the Jindois people once called *Non*." The woman grinned a minnow's mouth at the mention of *Non*, her teeth filmy and wet. Emmaline knew about Falls, but she had never heard of *Non*. "If you want to follow us home, that's up to you. But if you do, trail at a distance. Were one of your people to spot yeh traveling with us, they'd think we'd kidnapped yeh. So we won't be interacting with yeh during the trip. Though I wouldn't be surprised if we left behind some food from time to time." A quarter of a smile remained fixed on his face. His red eyebrows wriggled like caterpillars aflame. "Once we reach *Non*, there'll be a house, and food, and work. You're welcome to stay with us if you're so inclined."

Emmaline didn't reply. Making a decision at the present moment was beyond her. But the man nodded like they'd reached a suitable agreement. Then he stood and motioned for his children to do the same. Rising from their haunches, the boy gave Emmaline an entreating look, while the girl encouraged her with a beckoning wave. Before they could signal further, their parents ushered them away, and soon the foursome was walking through the forest, backs turned toward Emmaline, headed east.

She waited until they were nearly fifty yards off before rising. For lack of a better plan, she followed.

The man's name was Oostri. He had been brought to Dreyland from the island of Breek as a boy, in tow with his aunt, his last remaining living relative. At the time, it was common for poverty-stricken Breeks—meaning nine-tenths of the Breekish population—to sell themselves as indentured servants to Dreylanders. Over the years, the practice became fuzzy, so that by the time Oostri's aunt peddled their respective freedoms, it was difficult to say if she had auctioned off Oostri as a servant or a slave. Once in Dreyland, Oostri was treated as the latter, and he spent the remaining years of his boyhood tending to the capricious whims of a plantation princeling in northwest Tiderealm. He might have been miserable, had it not been his fortune to watch the Torquecans suffering and dying in the fields, which made his existence seem pleasant by comparison. Docile by nature, Oostri resigned himself to his fate, but then came the Sundering, when the ships that had for one hundred and seventy-five years bridged Harroland to Dreyland suddenly stopped arriving, some deep, dark magic having taken hold. Within weeks, a daring slave revolution arose, and for a time it was impossible to tell whether the oppressed would win a monumental victory or if the powers that be would snuff out the uprising with a terrible might. The end result was an uneasy compromise—the Dreylanders carved out a meager home state (Chineyaco, formerly Brine) for the Torquecans who demanded their freedom, and made indentured servants out of the ones who did not—but Oostri wasn't around to witness it: at an opportune moment, he fled into the mountains of Falls with a handful of fellow Breeks, and there made a new home, working the rocky soil that the conquering Harrolanders had forewent, living among the craggy peaks that called to mind his long-lost island home.

Oostri's children, Clay and Seywa, loved to hear their father retell his life's story, and they insisted whenever he reminisced that Emmaline join them, and bear witness. The mother, Shayo, who told no stories of her own—she hardly spoke, let alone spun yarns—always hovered at the periphery during Oostri's performances, seemingly preoccupied by household chores, but as time passed, Emmaline grew to believe that her presence served another purpose: she was there to ensure that Oostri didn't say too much. On those rare occasions when Oostri dipped his storytelling cup too deeply into the well of his shared past with Shayo, she would harrumph, or sweep her broom ever closer, or sing loud enough to disrupt, and Oostri, his eyes often heavy with grain alcohol, would laugh away his train of thought, and take up another.

Emmaline grew to love her new family, at least to the extent that she could, having lost her old one. The twins, Clay and Seywa, adopted her both as an older sister and as an arbiter of fair play: they happily turned over their many long-running disputes to her foreign judgement. She was wary of the role at first, thinking that to side with one was to alienate the other, but to her surprise she found that the loser was always as satisfied with her decision as the winner. The twins rewarded Emmaline's adjudicating prowess with long explorations of their mountain home. Initially, the mountain struck Emmaline as one in a seemingly endless chain of mica-flecked crags, but, with the children acting as her guide, she learned its secrets. Clay and Seywa showed her the powerful stream churning below the southern slope, the splotchy groupings of evergreens where the twins played and sometimes took shelter, and the animal tracks that occasionally, when followed, yielded glimpses of mountain creatures, wildcats and bighorn goats and jacket deer but more often ground squirrels and chatter dogs and junk rabbits. There were ostensibly neighbors on the nearby mountains but Emmaline never saw them, except for one time at a distance, when Clay pointed at the outline of three men walking the slope of a mountain miles away, and said, "There's Freskly, and Jojoy, and Yetts. They're Breekish like my dad. They escaped with him

17

from Tiderealm years ago." To which Emmaline nodded knowingly, having heard the story many times.

Oostri and Shayo each handled Emmaline differently. Oostri treated her with an affection that was a close relative to the affection he showed his children. Emmaline suspected that he had further reserves of this affection in store, but she kept them at bay by refusing to fully warm to his overtures. For every kind word that Oostri spoke, Emmaline responded with a gracious but detached deference, and in doing so staked out their relationship as transactional—hard work for food and a roof.

Shayo, Emmaline could tell, liked this about her. No kind words escaped from Shayo's mouth, but, on those rare occasions when Emmaline needed help, Shayo was first on the scene: she held a cold compress to Emmaline's forehead when Emmaline broke out in a sick fever; she saved food for Emmaline when Emmaline's chores went long; and she darned the holes in Emmaline's clothes without complaint, the same as she did for Clay and Seywa. Shayo watched Emmaline more carefully than the others, too, but there was no judgement in her attentions, only a guarded curiosity. After a few months Emmaline felt that Shayo knew her best of all, despite the fact that they never spoke.

Still, like the others, Shayo didn't know Emmaline's secrets. Emmaline was careful to keep those hidden away. The ones that resided in her thoughts were simple enough to conceal: Oostri was the only family member who asked about her past. He did this gingerly, making it clear that Emmaline didn't have to answer if she didn't want to. So she didn't. As time went by, he pried less and less, until there came a day when Emmaline felt certain that he had asked for the last time, and would leave any future revelations to her discretion.

Keeping the stone's existence a secret was a different matter. When Emmaline had first arrived in Falls, she buried the stone under a rock twenty yards behind the family's stone hut. But out of sight it plagued her mind, becoming, in its absence, a more distracting object than it had been in her hands. She worried that if she left it there she'd return to find it gone, dug up and carried away by a four-legged forager, or, worse, discovered by one of the two-legged creatures she lived with. So she dug it up.

Keeping it with her at all times brought its own set of challenges. More often than not she stored it in a pocket beneath her petticoat, then proceeded to pet it obsessively throughout the course of the day, checking to ensure that it was still there. On those rare occasions when she didn't keep it on her she hid it under the cot in her corner of the hut, but it called to her the same there as it had outside. Ultimately she decided to never put it down, a trying task but not as tiresome as letting the stone out of her sight.

Though she possessed the stone, Emmaline was too wary of its powers to try and summon the Deer King. But about one year after her arrival, finding herself alone by the stream, she attempted her father's trick. Turning the stone over and over in her hands and muttering the word *Dachahelu,* she watched with amazement as the child appeared, much changed from the last time she had seen him. His face was baby-fat full and his eyes were a hypnotic green, and on the crown of his head were tiny nubs—rough, wooden bumps. Most interesting of all was his comportment: for such a small babe, he appeared eerily possessed, a look of the ages in his eyes. While she watched the child, Emmaline felt the stone pulling west, toward Wolfresh. Unnerved, she stopped turning the stone over, and the boy disappeared.

After this first venture, she didn't try it again for weeks. But one day, alone in the hut, temptation got the better of her, and she summoned the boy once more. Within seconds the Deer King appeared, but so did the twins: they walked inside the hut the instant the rock revealed the young deity's face.

"What is that?" Clay asked with bald-faced curiosity when he saw the stone in her hands.

Emmaline glanced down. The boy had flickered away. In her hands remained a smooth, glassy, blue-grey stone, its color like a fractured sky.

"It's a stone," she replied. Emmaline's heart played a peculiar beat. She felt exposed, but also a sense of relief. Perhaps it was best if the family knew. Perhaps she would at last tell them her story.

The twins gathered round, full of dumb, sweet attention.

"Is it a special stone?" Seywa asked. Emmaline thought that Seywa's Harrish sounded like her father's, high-pitched and metallic. It stood in stark contrast to the earthy Massaporan Emmaline sometimes heard Seywa speaking with her mother.

"It is to me."

"Can I see it?" asked Clay.

Emmaline handed it over. Instantly Clay started turning the stone over and over in his hands. For a moment Emmaline was certain that the boy-king would appear, but, without the word being chanted, nothing happened. His curiosity slaked, Clay handed the stone to his sister.

Seywa held the stone with wary fingers, eyed it with a faint suspicion. "Mama says that bad people use magic stones to kill her god."

A lump formed in Emmaline's throat. She supposed that she had known on some unconscious level that Shayo was an adherent of the Deer King, but the reality of it startled her. Scrambled thoughts overran her mind: justifications excuses reasons apologies declarations. But she didn't reply, and the stone in Seywa's hand remained a stone.

"Here," Seywa said, handing it back. "I think yours is just a rock."

Emmaline nodded.

After revealing the stone to the twins, Emmaline began to feel, for the first time since arriving in Falls, like an outsider. She loved her adopted family no less, but now when she looked at them she couldn't help but focus on how she was different from them: her skin color was different, her accent was different, her body build was different, and, most of all, the fact that her father had devoted his life to preventing the rebirth of the warmongering god that Shayo's people worshipped was different.

Since her arrival, Emmaline had known that one day she would leave, but now plotting her departure felt urgent. Only she didn't know where to go and what to do. Or so she told herself. In truth, she knew exactly what she intended to do, only that the task ahead of her felt too monumental to begin.

She was haunted by dreams of her competing destinies. In her mind it seemed that she must either fulfill her father's unfinished task or avenge his death. The latter consumed her: she dreamed of the priest nonstop. In her dreams she was fearless, stalking the priest with a hound dog's abandon, howling for his blood, but no matter her bloodlust and want for revenge, it was he who dispatched her in the end, his size and experience too vast to overcome. Each time she awoke, she knew that she had already missed her best opportunity to end the priest's life, on the day that her father had died. But the frequency of the dreams made the attempt to find and kill him seem preordained, and the ensuing outcome, a matter of fate. Perhaps, she thought, dying at the priest's hands was her destiny.

But she also dreamt of the boy. The Deer King. Less frequent than her dreams of the priest, the ones of the boy were decidedly more varied in tone. In one of the dreams she was playing in her old front yard with her brother and father, when the boy suddenly joined them, frolicking with a feral abandon. He was older in the dream than he was in real life, and on his head were a pair of burgeoning antlers. Shortly after the boy appeared, Emmaline's father and brother vanished. Unable to find them, Emmaline turned on the boy, a rage like a tempest stirring up inside of her. She drew a knife from thin air and tackled the boy against the side of the cabin, but when she made to stab him he stopped her with his eyes, which were singed with a strange green fire.

Then she woke up.

In another she killed him. She found him waiting for her at the bottom of the mountain, presenting himself like an offering. She took a knife and slit his throat without a second thought. After doing so she discovered that she knew the way home. She returned to Haven and the old log cabin, but when she arrived the priest was waiting for her, and the dream ended as all her dreams with the priest ended.

In yet another dream she married the boy. He was a handsome teenager, and they stole away together deep into the Wolfresh woods, where a woman dressed in raven wings performed a ceremony that united their souls for all of eternity. They honeymooned in the belly of the earth, walking hand in hand into a cavern that knew no end. She awoke in a cold sweat the instant the last of the light from the cavern's entrance extinguished.

Time continued to pass. The summer beckoned, and with it, her fifteenth birthday. She decided that she would leave then. She took to sleeping outdoors in preparation for her travels. Clay and Seywa would often join her, thinking it a camping trip, and together the three of them would name the constellations, both the Harrish/Breekish and the Massaporan groupings. She winced when Seywa proudly pointed out *dachahelu*, the mighty antlers that filled the northern sky. She thought to show the twins the Bronze Titan holding his spear in the east, but when she looked closely, the stars resembled the priest, and she lost the urge. She wished that she could stick her hand into the firmament and stir the great starry soup, make the heavens anew. When they were finished naming the constellations, the twins would fall asleep and Emmaline would lay quietly, listening to them breathe. Then she would stay awake as long as possible, trying to remember her father's and brother's faces, trying to envision them in the stars.

One week before her birthday, she made her decision. She would go and search for the priest. It was a selfish decision, she knew, one that would likely end in her death, which, she had come to realize, was what she wanted most of all. When she had first arrived in Falls, she was distraught over the death of her father and brother, but it wasn't until Seywa said what she said about the stone that Emmaline's sadness overwhelmed her. She knew that she could never truly belong to a family that was sympathetic to the Deer King. There was nothing left for her in life but to meet her destiny, the same as Brutus and Joseph. She told herself that if she managed to kill the priest, she would hunt down the Deer King. But she was confident that death would take her before then.

The day of her fifteenth birthday arrived. Her intention was to run away in the afternoon—she often took a long walk then, and she doubted that her disappearance would be noted for some time—but near lunchtime Shayo yelled for Emmaline and the twins to come inside from tending the family garden, her voice laced with urgency. Hurrying inside, the three of them saw Shayo cradling Oostri's listless head in her lap, stroking the fiery filaments of his hair. Emmaline thought he was dead: his naturally pale pallor had turned ghostly white, and his lively eyes, the boiler of his personality, were cold and lifeless.

"What happened? What's wrong with him?" Emmaline asked Shayo, not understanding. When she had last seen him an hour ago, he had been fine. The twins, standing behind her, appeared concerned, but not altogether surprised.

"Old poison," Shayo replied. "From a long time ago. His master in Tiderealm made the house slaves drink it. The Silver Worm. It lies dormant, until it doesn't." She looked at Seywa.

"Do," she said, which meant daughter in Massaporan, "bring me the *olorusco*."

Seywa moved quickly, darting across the hut and removing a stone in the wall. Behind it, a small leather pouch. She brought it on swift feet to her mother.

Shayo opened the pouched and extricated a strange clot of leafy, purple-brown product. Still cradling Oostri's head, she firmly but delicately stuffed a sizeable amount of it into the corner of his gums. Seconds later, Oostri came to life: his eyes darted about the hut and landed on every person in turn, wild and grateful.

"Ah, the worm lives," he chuckled weakly when at last he found his voice. "Tasty, that," he continued, licking his lips before spitting a mushy glob of brown onto the floor. "But now I'll need to deaden the cravings. What *wiswake* we have is long expired, no doubt," he said, looking at Shayo.

Shayo's sad smile served as a response. Oostri sighed, then smiled. "It appears a trip is in store," he said to Emmaline and the kids.

Emmaline's confusion persisted. Shayo, noting it, addressed her. "When the *olorusco* enters the bloodstream, it takes the life out of the worm, lulls it into a deep slumber. Without the *olorusco,* your life belongs to the worm, who may keep you in bed for months on end or end your life. But the *olorusco* brings with it its own set of problems."

"'Tis a sweet leaf," cooed Oostri, "for a time."

Shayo continued stroking Oostri's hair, though her demeanor grew matter-of-fact. "It's best not to chew *olorusco*. Some men, once they have tasted it, desire nothing else for the rest of their days. It's why the masters in Tiderealm poisoned their house slaves. Then they could control them with the *olorusco*." With her free hand she pointed east. "But to live under the *olorusco's* spell for too long is to say goodbye to both normality and sanity. Such is the fate of Oostri's mountain brothers."

"They can't go into Wolfresh for the *wiswake* like I can," Oostri protested, defending them. "They don't have a Massaporan wife to escort them."

Shayo shrugged, dismissing the men with a wave of her hand. "It's not a life that they lead, roaming the mountains, half out of their minds. It's an existence, nothing more. Besides, you've offered them the *wiswake*. They don't want it."

Oostri said nothing to this. Emmaline looked closely at Oostri. His pupils had dilated to the size of the moon, and he seemed to hum with a strange, insectoid energy.

Shayo addressed Emmaline once more. "The *olorusco* makes men alert. On it, they can stay awake for days. But it also makes them passive, dazed. Over time it destroys one's sense of identity. When Oostri and the others escaped Tiderealm, they stole enough *olorusco* both to last the journey and to grow their own crops in Falls. Once they were here and the leaf was planted, the others continued with their habit. Only Oostri did not. He found me. And then, together, we procured the *wiswake*."

"At a cost," chimed Oostri.

"Yes," admitted Shayo. "At a cost. But I was glad to pay the price."

Quiet fell. The unspoken parts of the conversation hovered in the room like spirits.

"Where do you find the *wiswake*?" Emmaline asked. And then, before Shayo could reply, "And what is it, exactly?"

"*Wiswake* is a paste made from the wood of a tree of the same name that grows deep in the forests of Wolfresh. It stays fresh for six to eight months, then loses its efficacy. The silver worm rears its head only now and again, sometimes with gaps as short as two months and sometimes as long as five years in between. So we travel to Wolfresh only when necessary."

Emmaline couldn't help but ask the obvious question. "Why not live in Wolfresh, then?"

One of the spirits showed its face. "We are allowed to visit. But living there is not permitted."

Another quiet. The spirit flitted away.

"We'll leave in the morning," Oostri said, breaking the stillness. Somewhere behind his glassy gaze his mind was operating, trying to decide what was best for his family. "Eight days there, eight days back. We'll be home in…"

Shayo's shaking head cut him off. "No. If we all leave now, we'll lose the early summer harvest. You stay here, and take the *olorusco* as needed. Remember last time? Traveling agitates the worm, and, once the worm is agitated, you become more dependent on the leaf. So stay. Rest. The children will tend the crops, and take care of you. Won't you?" she asked, looking at the twins.

Emmaline wasn't certain if she was included with the children, but she nodded her head regardless. In her mind, she thought, *Good. It will be easier to run away once Shayo's gone.*

But then Shayo's gaze fell on her like a lighthouse on a ship. It was a penetrating stare, different than any look Shayo had given Emmaline before. The map of Emmaline's mind felt exposed. "Emmaline will travel with me to Wolfresh. She's nearly a woman now. Besides, she needs to visit Wolfresh. She needs to meet my people. Together, we'll make good time. Faster than if we all went. We'll be home in a matter of weeks."

4

They left together later that same afternoon, at the hour that Emmaline had planned to slip away. By nightfall they had traveled five miles. They set up camp on the slope of a stunted mountain, one of the dwarf crags that overlooked the heavy pinewood forests that marked Wolfresh's northeastern border.

Now that they were alone together, Shayo resumed her habit of not speaking to Emmaline, a courtesy that Emmaline extended to Shayo in turn. They danced a soundless dance of chores: gathering kindling for the fire, boiling water from a nearby stream, constructing a lean-to in the event the grumbling clouds to the south carried their complaints north. Sitting cross-legged by the fire, they shared salted strips of beef and a piping-hot sweet potato for supper. Then they fell asleep like logs.

They reached the forests of Wolfresh by mid-morning the following day. They traveled at a brisk pace, stopping only occasionally to sip water from leather canteens. Emmaline, who owned two outfits, had opted at the last moment to wear the buckskin dress that Shayo had given to her three months prior, rather than the tattered petticoat and gown that she had brought with her to Wolfresh. It turned out to be a wise decision. The dress was comfortable for traveling, and it fit better than the petticoat and gown, which had begun to look unseemly on her. On the inside of the dress was a hideaway pocket that Emmaline had sewn in secret. While they traveled, Emmaline grazed the pocket from time to time to feel the stone. She felt the stone's pull stronger than usual. She wondered if she might steal an opportunity to look at it somewhere along the way.

When they made camp later that evening, Shayo spoke to her for the first time since their departure. "I'm going hunting," she announced. Then she left, offering Emmaline no instructions. Emmaline watched silently as Shayo disappeared into a tangle of blood elms and dew oaks, the pines now behind them. The instant she was out of sight, Emmaline fished out the stone.

She wasted no time in summoning the boy, rotating the stone and chanting "*Dachahelu*" in a hushed but insistent voice. The boy appeared in his usual possessed state, verdant irises aflame. The stone, energized by the boy's presence, tugged Emmaline west. Continuing to chant, Emmaline glanced up and looked westward, wondering how close to the boy she might come if she continued on the journey with Shayo. When she glanced back down, she gave a start. Peering at her from behind the boy was an old woman cloaked in raven feathers.

She dropped the stone.

Emmaline hadn't yet recovered from the shock of seeing the old woman when Shayo returned from the hunt, a pair of tan, long-legged rabbits slung over her shoulder. Emmaline sensed that Shayo knew that something was amiss, but Shayo said nothing, only went about the work of dressing the rabbits for the meal. Emmaline did her best to act normal. She helped Shayo prepare the meal, skewering the rabbits and rotating them over the fire, though throughout, the vision of the feather-cloaked woman plagued her mind. It seemed that Shayo would let the matter pass unmentioned—keeping quiet was in her character, after all—but when Emmaline took her first bite of rabbit meat, Shayo addressed the mood in a roundabout fashion.

"Considering running away again?"

Emmaline nearly choked on the rabbit. She wondered how long Shayo had suspected her plans; she wondered if Shayo had known back in Falls. Emmaline recovered quickly, however, and when she replied, a note of defiance crept into her voice. "And if I am? I'm not yours to keep."

Shayo didn't respond right away. Instead, she took a bite of rabbit and stared into the distance. The stars were flaring into existence; it seemed to Emmaline as if Shayo were gazing at *dachahelu*, searching for an answer there.

"I know," she responded at last.

They finished the meal. Emmaline supposed that that was that, and nothing more would be said of it, but moments after Emmaline licked the last of the rabbit juice clean from her lips, Shayo spoke again. "Stay with me until I have the *wiswake* in my possession. That's all I ask of you." Her voice sounded clean and cold, like falling snow.

This time it was Emmaline's turn to stare into the distance. Her eyes lit upon the Titan's spear. She resented that she garnered no comfort from it, that it offered her no sense of who she was as a person.

"I will," she answered. After all that Shayo and her family had done for her, it was the only answer that she could give.

On the fourth day of their travels, after a rainy night that had tried Emmaline's spirits, they came upon a Massaporan village. Shayo spotted it first, pointing at a smattering of rectangular wood and clay houses a couple hundred yards to the northwest. They might have skirted it and continued on their way, but seconds after spotting the village, a Massaporan family spotted them. The family, returning to the village after an early morning outing, approached.

Shayo offered up pleasantries to the family. They weren't reciprocated. The man of the family, who looked like a large, leathery beetle, growled at Shayo in harsh Massaporan, and scowled at Emmaline. What initially sounded like complaints evolved into a harangue. Emmaline grew increasingly uncomfortable. Shayo had stopped responding and seemed to be taking a measure of pleasure in the man's anger. The man appeared on the verge of combustion when Shayo rolled her arm over and presented him with the underside of her wrist. Seeing the tattoo there—a series of six connected black diamonds, strung three to a side and separated by a perfect black circle—the man gasped, as did his family. Their faces turned skeletal white, and they hurried away, muttering what were either apologies or frightened curses.

"Why did they react like that to your tattoo?" Emmaline asked as the family fled. Shayo had multiple tattoos, tribal symbols all. Emmaline had never suspected that the one on the underside of her wrist bore special significance.

"The six diamonds signify that I'm the friend of a powerful person. The black circle represents my exile from the Massaporan community. I'm allowed to travel through Wolfresh, but I'm not allowed to build a home, and no Massaporan is permitted to offer me food and shelter."

"But your friend, wouldn't he…"

"My friend is a she. And no. Seeing as how she's the one who exiled me."

Emmaline wanted to ask additional questions, but Shayo signaled that they needed to move on. By the time they stopped at midday to eat, the window for asking questions had passed.

They moved deeper into the heart of Wolfresh. The unrelenting woods dominated the terrain: towering blood elms shadowed every inch of land with their leafy crowns, massive dew oaks hoarded terra firma with trunks as thick as boulders, while underneath the forest canopy saplings pushed and prodded at each other like jealous siblings, competing for space and recognition. Massaporan villages appeared with increasing frequency, camouflaged in the timber. Now and again Emmaline and Shayo were forced to deal with the Massaporans themselves. The result was always a variation of their first encounter: Shayo carried on contentious conversations, and Emmaline endured sneers and scowls; then Shayo flashed her tattoo, and their harassers departed posthaste. Emmaline hadn't thought to be frightened before she came to Wolfresh, but now that she was here, she realized how naïve she had been. The Massaporans hated her. She wondered how her father had ever operated in a land so hostile to his existence.

On the seventh day they spotted yet another village, smaller than most. Emmaline supposed that they would skirt it as they had the others, but instead Shayo led them to the edge of the village. A lanky, long-boned Massaporan with a horse's face greeted them.

"It's good to see you, Shayo," the man said in Harrish, eschewing Massaporan. He had an aloof, regal bearing.

"And you, Uncle," she replied.

The man looked at Emmaline, neither disdain nor approval in his eyes. "This one isn't Breekish."

"No, she isn't. Oostri is still alive, if you're probing. As are your niece and nephew."

Shayo's uncle nodded noncommittally, as if Shayo had asked him a question that couldn't be answered instead of telling him a fact. Shayo smiled, continued, "They still speak of the honey apples you gave them the last time we visited."

"Honey apples *are* delicious," he said, looking away. "Now tell me who the girl is."

Shayo switched to Massaporan. Though Emmaline didn't understand what she said, something about Shayo's tone sent a shock of fear through her system. Emmaline looked from Shayo to the man, whose eyes thrashed hard and then went still, like a fish caught in a net.

"Let's go, then," the man said.

"I need *wiswake*," Shayo demanded with authority. Shayo had an air about her of one battle won, and another on the verge of being fought. Emmaline's mind swirled in confusion, trying to adapt to the subtle changes taking place.

Shayo's uncle nodded but didn't reply. He turned and led them into the village.

The village was bruised from a recent storm, a lightning-struck dew oak having toppled into the midst. Fallen from the northwest, the massive tree cleaved the village in half, starting at ten o'clock on the dial and landing at four. Two houses had been smashed in its wake, pressed flat like trampled clover. The storm's detritus—scattered tree limbs, castaway leaves—lay around the village in an embryonic pattern, the peculiar artistry of a storm god. Massaporans moved like dreams around the wreckage, reinterpreting their daily lives with a seamless grace. If they glanced Emmaline's way they acted as if they didn't see her. She assumed it was because Shayo's uncle was their guide.

Shayo's uncle led them to the heart of the tree, where a gaggle of Massaporan children frolicked, the lot of them so thick that at first Emmaline didn't notice the gaping hole bored into the center of the colossal dew oak. The hole was large enough for humans to enter, which they did. To Emmaline' wonderment, inside of the tree was a corridor, straight and dark and leading to the roots. Emmaline glanced behind her as she disappeared into the tree and saw the children staring after her, their curious faces blurring into a smudgy halo.

They pressed forward into the void. Somewhere ahead, near the root system, shone a single, flickering light. They picked up speed, proverbial moths. In the back of the tree, resting on a wicker chair lit by a candle atop a tree-stump table, sat an old woman cloaked in raven feathers.

Emmaline gasped. The woman found her with shriveled-prune eyes. Emmaline considered running, but before she could, Shayo's uncle grabbed her by the arm. The woman lifted a crooked finger and pointed it at her. She spoke with a raspy trill.

"I've seen you before."

5

They took the stone. Emmaline refused to give it up willingly, so Shayo's uncle—whose name was Prala—patted her with his big hands until he discovered the hideaway pocket. She curled into the hard kernel of herself while he searched her, glaring icily at Shayo, who refused to look her way.

The old woman gave a cry of joy when Prala handed the stone over. She stood up and spread her raven-feather wings in an ecstatic arc, before cupping her hands around the stone and bringing it closer to the candlelight. "Doido, you fool," she said as she studied it, a laugh like a popping bubble escaping her lips. When she was finished, she stored the stone somewhere in her great mess of feathers, the plumage shimmering obsidian in the candlelight. Emmaline strained to see, but in the dark, she couldn't tell if the feathers were an actual cloak or an extension of the woman's arms.

The old woman spoke to Shayo in the Massaporan tongue. Before Shayo could reply, Prala chimed in. Shayo's face went dark. "That may have been what I said, but it wasn't what I meant," she responded to the both of them in Harrish. "The stone is the gift. Not the girl."

"If you're speaking in Harrish, you must want the girl to hear you," the old woman said. "Go ahead, then. Speak to her."

Shayo turned to Emmaline. Emmaline, who had desired nothing more these last few minutes than to level Shayo with a withering stare, now jerked her head away, unable to meet her eyes.

Shayo's voice was a pounding waterfall. "I've known that you had the stone—what we Massaporans call the Doido pebble—for some time now. I knew even before Seywa told me that you were hiding a secret rock. I watched you bury it in our backyard, and I watched the way it tormented you after you dug it up. I had planned to steal it from you, but after you dug it up, you never let it out of your sight. Near the end, I knew that if you kept it much longer, it would lead to your death."

The candlelight leapt into the darkness, aided by a draft of wind. It changed its mind quick enough to save itself, holding fast to the wick and existence.

Shayo continued. "So I brought you with me to Wolfresh. To deliver the Doido pebble to *Fecheholo,* in exchange for *wiswake* and in the hope that my family's exile from Wolfresh might be brought to an end. But whether or not my wishes are granted..." she turned away from Emmaline, and glowered at the old woman, "...I expect the *Fecheholo* to let you go. After all, she has no reason to keep you."

The old woman cackled. "No reason?" Her smile was a gash of teeth. She motioned at Emmaline. "This young viper you nurtured in your nest, do you know who her father was?"

Shayo didn't blink. "The Stoneman, most likely."

"*Most likely.* Of course it was the Stoneman. And do you know how many newborn Deer Kings this particular Stoneman ushered off the earth?"

Shayo didn't reply.

"Ninety-three. Ninety-three suckling pups with the potential to restore the world to its rightful state. Ninety-three who would have allowed the Massaporan people to show their might once more. But this young woman's father killed them all." The old woman suddenly turned to Emmaline. "What is your name, whelp?"

She considered holding her tongue to spite the old woman, but the words spilled out. "Emmaline. Emmaline Rain."

"Rain," the old woman echoed. "Rain to wash the Massaporan people away. Your people sing a song about it, don't they?" she asked Emmaline. A broken tune formed on her lips. *"And if antlers sprout, don't go messing about, just summon the rain, it best be over."* She cawed hoarsely when the stanza was finished, deliberately grating. Taking her sweet time, she at last turned back to Shayo. "But of course my daughter would think it right to save the child of our oppressor. My daughter, who sleeps with an ugly creature from across the sea, and who bears half-blood children."

Shayo didn't respond. Even in the scant light, Emmaline could see the hurt in her face, her pain exposed like a sedimentary rock shorn to reveal an inner layer.

"A choice, then," the old woman pronounced when it was clear that Shayo wouldn't respond. "In exchange for Doido's pebble, you may take the girl with you when you leave; or, I will end your exile. With the exile over, you and your family may return to Wolfresh, where you'll be cared for, and where the *wiswake* will always be in reach. I'll brand you so that you and your family's presence will never be questioned, so long as you all shall live."

Shayo was impossible to read. Her body had gone rigid, and her tongue, it seemed, was captive inside her mouth, a prisoner bound by a tangled knot of conflicting thoughts. Seconds passed. The old woman waited patiently. Happily. The seconds grew interminable to everyone but her. At last, Prala spoke a hushed word to Shayo in Massaporan, and it broke her from the spell.

"End the exile," Shayo said clearly for all to hear. Her face had changed into that hard and inscrutable mask that Emmaline had so often seen her wear. A face that claimed ownership for the decisions she made. A face now turning Emmaline's way.

"Do what you want with the girl," Shayo said.

Shayo left later that day. Emmaline, bound by ropes to the crest of the fallen dew oak, nearly missed her departure. From a distance, she couldn't see Shayo's altered tattoo, nor the jar of *wiswake* in Shayo's hand; she only saw the fleeting, familiar stride of the woman she had followed twice through the forests of Wolfresh, vanishing into those same woods without her.

She thought after Prala tied her to the tree that she was to be subjected to the ridicule and scorn of the Massaporan villagers. But all that first day the adults avoided her. She might have believed herself invisible had she not seen the expanding orbit her presence engendered; Massaporans who otherwise succumbed to the tree's gravitational pull were repelled by its crest and the creature tied there. By and large the children followed the adults' lead, although there were times when Emmaline felt eyes resting on her, and she would look up to see a child take flight, scrambling back into the fold of friends who had dared them. But for the most part everyone kept their distance.

As she sat there, she couldn't help but wonder what the old woman—the *Fecheholo*—had in store for her. She tried to wrap her mind around the woman with the raven feathers. Who was she? What did *Fecheholo* mean? How was she connected to the Deer King? Had the old woman been the one to orchestrate Joseph's death? Her father's failure? She prayed to her father, but he was an ineffectual god; he couldn't answer her prayers now that he was dead, just as he hadn't answered her questions when he was alive. While pondering these unknowables, she dug at the earth with her nails and brought the soil to her lips, hoping to taste the truth. She was certain that she would die but determined to sate her ravenous mind before doing so.

Late that evening Prala brought her dinner, a brown soup with carrots, corn, and chunks of squirrel. She wolfed it down. Full, her mind slowed, no longer racing to the end of things but lingering in the present. She took closer note of her surroundings. Though her vantage point was obscured by the fallen tree, she could see a smattering of the Massaporan houses, and around the houses the miscellanea of daily life: stretched and drying animal hides, kettles, tools, earthenware, cooking fires, strange wooden toys, and other items that she didn't have enough experience to place. Excepting small differences, she thought that the Massaporan village wasn't entirely unlike Mossbane. But then her vision snagged on a peculiarity, one that, once noticed, caught her eye again and again: a symbol resembling an incomplete triangle with branching lines pouring out of both sides, carved onto a myriad of surfaces: the house logs, the earthenware pots, the tanning hides; she noticed it nearly everywhere, finding it even when she glanced down the trunk of the fallen dew oak and saw the symbol carved into the bark no more than eight feet away from her.

She was scanning the village for additional carvings of the symbol when the Deer King approached. Emmaline turned her head and there he was, approaching from the base of the fallen dew oak, flanked by scores of villagers. It was the end of the day: out on the western horizon, the sun was taking deep bites of the earth, its jaw disappearing by degrees. In this burgeoning darkness, the color of the boy's eyes intensified: his otherworldly greens burned like an eternal flame. When he was ten feet away, he fixed his pupils on her. She refused to wilt under the heat of his stare, though in doing so she began to feel nauseous, as if strung between this world and another.

It took Emmaline a moment to recognize that the villagers surrounding the Deer King were staring at her too, their eyes a pale reflection of the Deer King's verdant greens. Theirs was a vicious, hungry look, hatred tinged with impending violence. They looked as if they wanted to tear her apart, but were waiting on a signal, perhaps from the boy. A deep, animal fear welled up inside of Emmaline. She had made her peace with death in the previous months, but this was something different, a fear not of death but of being devoured, mutilated, savaged. Panicked, her mind began to race, so that she lost sense of who she was, and instead became a conduit for fear itself: the very core of her personality disintegrated into a screaming, thrashing, desperate entity, as she attempted, by any means necessary, to free herself from the ropes and run away.

When she came back into herself, everything had changed. The villagers were dispersing, drifting away into the gloaming, and standing beside her was the boy. His green eyes had adopted a human hue; they were no longer the spirit-world irises of seconds ago. Not only that, his stare was beseeching, that of a toddler in need. He held out his arms to her. Too bewildered to do anything else, she picked him up.

Emmaline's racing heart was hesitant to slow. She was nonplussed by the boy: it was difficult to square the harmless toddler in her arms with the frightening deity of moments ago with an army at his back. But the further he nestled into the crook of her arms, the harder it was to stay panicked. In a manner of minutes, the Deer King fell sleep. Emmaline eased to the ground, trying her best not to wake him. She leaned her back against the fallen dew oak. Slowed her breathing. She thought she might fall asleep herself, but each time she edged toward unconsciousness, the reality of who she was holding kept her tethered to the waking world. At one point, the boy stirred ever so slightly. Without thinking, she soothed him by running her hand over the top of his head. She felt the nubs there, firm little mounds. They jarred her senses. She sat there bewildered, staring at the boy and then up at the blue-black sky, where high above, *dachahelu* stretched across the firmament, certain of its position in the pantheon.

The night deepened. From time to time, Emmaline succumbed to sleep, drifting into its dreamy recesses, but never for long. The boy, cozily wedged into the crook of her arm, remained there each time the tide of slumber brought her back ashore. Her interims of unconsciousness lengthened. After a particularly long spell, she awoke and sensed a pair of eyes upon her. She strained into the night and thought she saw a glimmering spell of feathers. But as she tried to focus, they disappeared into the black.

Sleep took her under one last time. When next she awoke, the forest was streaked with the playful colors of the morning sun, and the boy was gone.

When the sun was at its highest point, Prala brought her a meal of yams and ground nuts. Like the day before, he was silent throughout the meal, but, to her surprise, when she had finished eating, he untied her from the dew oak and said, "Follow me."

He led her back into the dark heart of the tree. Waiting in the same wicker chair at the tree's end was the old woman. The old woman dismissed Prala with a wave of her hand. Then she stared at Emmaline with a burning intensity, as if trying to scour her brain. Emmaline, feeling uneven from the events of the night before, quickly grew uncomfortable, and averted her gaze. She tried to steady her nerves for the trial to come. But it was difficult with the old woman's stare singeing her like hot coals.

At last the old woman spoke. "You might have wrung the boy's neck last night. Finished your father's job."

Emmaline was stunned that the thought hadn't occurred to her. But she knew immediately that she wouldn't have done it. Killing a child, even the god-child of her enemy, wasn't in her, despite her previous plans. But she kept these thoughts to herself, and didn't answer.

The old woman harrumphed. Then she sprung to her feet with a startling quickness and hopped toward Emmaline, sleek feathers whispering. She stuck her timeworn face in Emmaline's, and, with a breath that smelled of cloves and garlic, demanded answers. "Tell me about this priest, girl. The one that killed your father. I hear he's as tall as an Impossible mountain and as ruthless as a feeding badger. But you got the better of him, or so the trees tell me. Share your thoughts."

Emmaline was stunned. "How did you know?"

The old woman smacked sandpaper lips. "What? You don't believe that the trees whisper secrets in my ear? I know that two plus two equals four, whelp. That stone belonged to the Stoneman before the priest came to take it away. The Stoneman was your father. Stands to reason that since the priest returned to Olgard without Doido's pebble, and that since your father is dead, and that since I stole the stone from you, I'm left to assume that you bested the priest. The question is: how?"

Emmaline spat out the truth. "I climbed on the roof of our house and dropped a chimney stone on his head."

The old woman's eyes lit up like a stoked fire. "Ha! Not bad for a she-bitch with Harrish bloodlines. That's what we'll do, then. I'll set you on top of a mud-log house with a chimney stone, and hope your aim is true when the bastard rides by."

Emmaline had difficulty telling whether or not the old woman was being sarcastic.

"He's coming here? The priest?"

"He's not *coming* here, whelp. He's been here. Off and on for nearly ten months now."

Startled and confused by the news, Emmaline glanced behind her.

"Not the cavernous heart of this specific dew oak," the old woman snapped, whipping around and returning to the wicker chair, feathers rustling as she went. "Wolfresh. When he returned to Olgard, he took the last remaining stone from the temple, so he thinks he knows how to find the boy. He's visited us before, but I threw him off the scent. But I fear he's smartened up. He'll return soon enough."

"Soon enough? Why hasn't he found the boy already? Doesn't the stone show him where the boy is?"

"Of course it does. But I have my ways."

Emmaline couldn't stop from asking questions. "How do you keep the boy hidden?"

"Sleight of hand. The offering of imitation apples. You wouldn't have found him, either."

"I wasn't looking for him."

The old woman made a pug's face in the flickering candlelight. "Of course you weren't, whelp. You're innocent, you. You're only the daughter of a man with the blood of ninety-three babes on his hands." The old woman rubbed her hands together near the flickering candle, as if cleaning them in the fire. "You may not believe me, but I liked your father. Mortal enemy of my people or not, he had a workmanlike manner about him that made his baby butchering nearly tolerable. He didn't lord his power, or take outward joy in his profession, or spout nonsense about that bronze god of yours. No, he simply slit babies' throats and then went on his way, the way a Stoneman should."

Emmaline's ears burned hot. The old woman's words danced around her like taunting demons.

"You think I'm joking, but it's true," the old woman continued. She reached into the darkness and conjured a *bittirinu*—a sweetened roll of tobacco—from beneath the candle. Satisfied with its look and smell, she lit one end in the flame, and took a sweet, slow drag. "I even helped him over the last few months of his life. When a woman gave birth, I was there to offer assistance. He thought me a midwife. I would encourage him: *'Oh yes, this one's giving birth to a little devil, I'm sure of it.'* Duplicitous, no doubt, and perhaps it makes me guilty of deicide, but I believe the god that matters will forgive me in the end. By watching your father, I was able to plan his downfall. Like all good subjugators, he wanted to believe that those he oppressed understood the necessity of it. I convinced him that we did. So he confided in me. He told me that he intended to make his son the next Stoneman. And I used that information to bring that darling little god you held last night into existence."

"You killed my brother?" The words tasted like burnt ash in Emmaline's mouth.

"I did."

"How?"

The old woman leaned forward and rested her arms on the front of her legs, the *bittirinu* dangling from inattentive fingers. "With cold, sharp steel, whelp. How else? His blood ran hot over my hands. I relished it."

"Why didn't my father stop you?" Emmaline asked, her voice neutral and cold.

"He was otherwise indisposed. Of course, we intended to kill your father as well, but he's a resourceful fellow. Still, the babe lived. That was all that really mattered." The old woman smiled at Emmaline with tobacco-stained teeth. "But enough about that. What's done is done."

A terrible fury overtook Emmaline. She sized the old woman up and realized that she could end her life if she desired. Her body flooded with relief: at last, she had found the right person to kill. But when she moved to wrap her hands around the old woman's throat, the old woman responded by muttering an unintelligible word. The instant Emmaline's hands found the old woman's neck, Emmaline began to choke: the air fled her lungs as if commanded, and, no matter how hard she struggled, she was unable to draw another breath. The old woman watched Emmaline struggle with a disinterested air, savoring the *bittirinu*. Emmaline thought she would soon black out, but then the old woman flicked the ash off the end of the *bittirinu* and touched Emmaline on the arm, muttering another unintelligible command. The pressure around Emmaline's throat released.

"No more of that," the old woman said as Emmaline gasped for air. "Your anger may be honest, but dealing with it is a waste of my time and energy. Plus, I have a fondness for killing Harrish she-whelps, so don't tempt me."

Emmaline tried not to show her shock. What the old woman had done was magic, pure and simple. Emmaline found her breath and, composing herself as best as she could, asked the first question that came to mind, one that she thought might shed some light on the old woman's true nature. "Shayo called you *Fecheholo*. What does that mean?"

The old woman took another drag off the *bittirinu*. The ember cast a fleeting light on her wizened face, which resembled a tremored ground exposed to a moment's sunlight. Below, black feathers glinted.

"Do you expect to live long, whelp?" the old woman asked, ignoring Emmaline's question.

"No," Emmaline replied.

The old woman grinned in appreciation of Emmaline's honesty. "Odds are you're right. You may catch me in a foul mood one day soon and I'll do the deed. Or perhaps the priest will arrive and I'll offer you up as a gift. Or—worst of all for you—the boy may tire of your presence and permit our people to tear you to shreds. But I've lived too long to take solace in odds. So I'll keep my secrets to myself, lest the day comes when you use them against me. If your priest comes, be sure to ask him. He may tell you just before he cuts your throat."

Emmaline brushed aside the death threats. "Do you have a different name? One other than *Fecheholo*?"

"No," the old woman spat. The look on her face appeared to vacillate between growing tired of Emmaline and being amused by her.

"What about the boy? Does the boy have a name other than *Dachahelu*?" Emmaline knew the segue was jarring, awkward, but she had to ask the questions that she wanted answered while she had the chance, before the old woman sent her away.

The old woman's eyes narrowed. "Yes, he does. Though it's of no importance." She paused. "The boy's name is Notel."

Footsteps ached against the floor of the dew oak. Prala, seemingly summoned, had returned. His long, thin shadow devoured Emmaline's, the dark floor of the tree turning darker still.

"Tie her back up," the old woman said to her brother. "She was of no help with the priest. Plus she tried to choke me, which was of no consequence, although her questions were a damn nuisance." The old woman licked her lips. Eyed Emmaline devilishly. "Be sure to bring the boy to her tonight, and every night thereafter. Gods are fickle creatures. He'll grow tired of her. I'm certain of it."

The Massaporans gathered again that evening. The same villagers that had spent the day pretending Emmaline didn't exist coalesced in a demoniac mass behind the child with green-flame eyes, only to disperse into the expanding night when the child's eyes went soft and he ran to Emmaline for comfort.

Tonight, she tried to make a study of him. It was clear that he wasn't like other children, for reasons above and beyond the obvious. He moved with a feral grace befitting a young animal of the woods, not a human child of one year, and the strength residing in his small frame was apparent even when he slept, the latent power like an unspoken threat against anyone who drew near. His hair was a thick, rich brown thatched with the debris of the woods, sticks and leaves and skittering insects, though on him the debris had a crown-like rather than a desultory effect. The antler nubs on the crown of his head poked through his hair like stony mounds. Emmaline desired to see his green-flame eyes, but now that he was in her arms he wouldn't open them. She told herself that if she stayed awake she would be rewarded with a glimpse in the morning, but sleep came like a thief in the night and stole away her willpower.

When the sun rose, he was gone.

On the third day, Prala untied her from the tree. "The *Fecheholo* says you are free to move about the village as you please. But don't be mistaken: if you try to run away, we will stop you. And if you're too troublesome, I will kill you." He refused to look at her when he spoke.

When she wandered the village, the Massaporans treated her the same: their eyes took flight when she approached. Only the children made eye contact, but those daring enough to do so battled their conscience in the process, and in their subsequent guilt spurned her all the more. The little ones whose eyes could not be corralled were ushered away from Emmaline. She walked the village like a ghost.

Or so she thought. Bored, she began tallying the strange triangle-shaped symbol carved into myriad surfaces around the village. Upon locating the fortieth—carved into a blood elm on the village edge—she ran her fingers over its many branching lines. She was lost in curiosity when a Massaporan man bearing a broomstick thwacked her hard on the offending forearm. Stunned, she cried out in pain. The indifferent Massaporan thwacked her once more while saying "*rute, rute*," which she knew meant "no." She stopped immediately and looked at the man, who, like the others, refused to meet her eyes. He continued threatening her with the broomstick until she moved away.

She spent the remainder of the day nursing her wounds. Before sundown, Prala brought her a meal of venison and charred squash. The meal surprised her: she had assumed the Massaporans forewent venison for religious reasons. She wanted to ask Prala why deer wasn't forbidden, but his granite demeanor dissuaded her. Chewing on the venison, it dawned on Emmaline that the old woman was the only person in the village who cared to acknowledge her existence. She was so lonely that the thought of being called before the *Fecheholo* again seemed appealing.

In due time dusk arrived. On cue, the nightly ritual recommenced. Emmaline waited for the same scene to play itself out, but tonight the boy's flaming green eyes refused to temper. The Massaporans grew even more frenzied with each passing second. Emmaline, unnerved, didn't notice at first that the boy's gaze was directed not at her, but at an unseen threat in the woods. By then the villagers were a bellicose mass, screaming and gnashing their teeth and making what Emmaline could only assume were terrible threats in the Massaporan tongue. Convinced that she was seconds away from being torn to shreds, Emmaline screamed the boy's name: "Notel!" Hearing her, the boy's consciousness shifted. The flames in his eyes disappeared. He looked around, and, for the first time that night, saw Emmaline clearly.

He rushed to her arms.

She tried to settle the boy down, but tonight he was restless and distracted. She, too, was agitated: fearing for her life had taken a toll. In an attempt to calm herself as much as the boy, she began singing soft lullabies. Without thinking, she launched into "Best Be Over." Hearing the song, the boy reared back and fixed her with a spirit-world stare. Up close, she could see that the green flames in the boy's eyes were the spirits of past Deer Kings flickering in and out of view. The visions were mesmerizing: the respective Deer Kings would flicker into existence on the periphery of the boy's irises, war across their expanse, and then disappear into the pupils' black wells. The same physical characteristics that distinguished regular men also differentiated the Deer Kings, but the similarities—an imposing antler rack strewn with greenery, spirit-world eyes, and a terrifying intensity—left no doubt that these different reincarnations originated from the same source.

The images were so hypnotic that Emmaline was slow to recognize that the boy's comportment had changed. He bristled with a dangerous energy, despite the fact that she had stopped singing the song almost immediately. She tried stroking his hair, but he jerked away from her with an animal violence, and, when she didn't let go, seemed on the verge of attacking her. In desperation, she cooed his name, "Notel, Notel, Notel."

Saying his name worked like a charm. His rigid body softened in her arms. She watched with muted fascination as the visions in his eyes retreated into an invisible world.

The night wore on. Emmaline continued to chant the boy's name. Under its spell, the boy further relaxed, and at last fell asleep. Like the previous two nights, Emmaline struggled to fall asleep, but, unlike the other nights, when at last she did, this time hers was a deep slumber.

She awoke to a pale white sunrise. As expected, the boy was gone. She was adjusting to the waking world when she noticed a hubbub near the front of the village.

The priest who had killed her father was trotting into the village on horseback.

6

Emmaline crouched beside the dew oak and tried her best to stay out of sight.

The priest waited on an audience to form. In the meantime, he trotted the Rugarder back and forth, stirring up dust. The villagers obliged his wishes, emerging from their wood and clay houses to pay the priest his due. There was something of a song and dance routine to the proceedings, a sense that both sides had been through this before.

Once everyone was assembled, the priest held aloft a blue-grey stone. Doido's pebble. The priest looked the master of equipoise sitting astride his horse: no emotion seeped from his countenance. But when at last he spoke, anger flared on his tongue.

"Go on!" he roared. "Bring me another imposter!"

Murmurings in the Massaporan tongue. Emmaline wondered if the villagers understood what the priest had said. She searched the crowd for both Prala and the old woman. They both spoke Harrish, so she assumed one of the two of them would speak up if present. But they were nowhere to be seen.

The murmurings quieted. From somewhere in the heart of the crowd a man walked forward holding the hand of a bawling, snot-nosed child. A scrawny half-formed thing. Definitely not the Deer King. Upon reaching the priest, the man picked up the boy and held him aloft in a sacrificial pose. The priest snatched the boy from the man's outstretched arms like the boy was a rag doll. Sensing what was about to happen, Emmaline looked away, stricken with horror. Thoughts of her father raced like wildfire across her mind: had he too been a butcher like this? The reality of her father's occupation hit her in a way that it never had before. Staring at the ground, she waited for the cries of protest from the crowd, but they never came. A distant thump. When she lifted her head, she saw the boy lying bloodied and lifeless on the ground, and the priest wielding a blood-dripping dagger.

The priest fixed the crowd with a wild-eyed stare. His black beard flowed from his face in a brambly torrent. He looked like he would murder every Massaporan present if he could. He was so terrifying that Emmaline feared for the villagers, despite the fact that they had an overwhelming advantage in numbers.

"No more games!" he shouted. "Now, bring me the real boy! Bring me the Dachahelu!"

The villagers didn't move. They stood as placid before the priest as they had stood frenzied in front of Emmaline, the only similarity being the peculiar power they possessed when coalesced. The priest, angered, loosed a war cry of frustration, "AAAAAHHHHHHHH!" Then he began to turn the stone over and over in his hands. Emmaline heard the word *Dachahelu* rumbling off his lips like a rockslide. A few moments later he scowled. "Damn sorcery!" he shouted, but he cut his words short, returning to the chant. Without warning he began steering the horse in wild, unpredictable patterns, all the while staring at the rock like it was a portent he couldn't quite divine. The villagers ebbed and flowed with the animal's movements, careful to stay out of harm's way. In a flash, the priest spurred the horse into a gallop. The beast knifed through the villagers as it headed directly toward Emmaline.

Emmaline was too stunned to move. Her heart seized into a fist as the beast drew closer, the sound of thunder in its hooves. The priest sat atop the animal like a statue of the Bronze Titan on *Felling Day,* war and death etched in every crease and corner of his face. But then, to Emmaline's surprise, the priest veered away without registering her presence, guiding the Rugarder down the length of the tree until he reached the gaping hole in the tree's center.

Once there, the priest dismounted. He stared at the blue-grey stone, perplexed, pondering whether or not to take the fateful step inside. But before he could make up his mind, the *Fecheholo* emerged from the aperture.

The old woman looked chimerical in the light of day, an ancient being from another time and place. The feathers, it turned out, were indeed sewn into a cloak, but on the old woman they looked as real as if they had sprouted from her skin. The old woman's wrinkles were pond ripples, her posture ramrod. Standing beside the priest, the old woman was so small that she barely appeared to exist; only this contrast magnified her stature, for in her presence the priest stood stupefied, daunted by the sheer audacity of her presence.

"Do you know who I am?" the old woman asked the priest.

"Yes," the priest replied. "You're the *Fecheholo.* The Raven Queen." His voice was low and deep, like thunder in a valley. His black eyes were burning coal. He looked discomfited by the old woman's presence, but also somewhat unsurprised, as if he had expected her all along.

"Good. You may look like an ogre, but it's good to know you're not as stupid as one. Or perhaps I'm assuming too much. Another question then. Are you stupid enough to try and kill me?"

"If I must," the priest replied, nervousness in his voice. "All said, I would rather you hand over the boy." He motioned at the dew oak. "Is he inside the tree?"

"Yes, ogre, there is a boy inside this tree. But we've already given you a different boy, have we not? Why do you need this one as well?"

"You must give me the *Dachahelu*. This has gone on for too long. If I return to Olgard without killing the boy, they'll send an army of thousands to murder every Massaporan in Wolfresh. Your people will be wiped from the face of Drey…Tsadanali."

The old woman laughed, a hearty cackle. "Why would they do that, ogre? We have killed no Stoneman. That was *you*."

"You killed his son."

Another laugh, this one harsher and louder than the last. "Yes, I did do that. But killing a young Havenese boy does not break the pact."

"You are harboring a demon, *Fecheholo*. You must turn him over. You break the *Wolfresh-Potter Accord* by keeping him from us. You know as well as I do that the boy must die."

The old woman grinned a vile grin. "I know many things, priest. I know that in the *Temple of the Bronze Titan* there were once two blue-grey stones, but now there are none. I know that you are Kern, the keeper of the Saving Stones, and that it is your job to safeguard the traitor Doido's portents. I know that you lost one of the stones after retrieving it from the Stoneman Brutus Rain from Mossbane, whose son I killed. I know that you returned to Olgard and took the other stone from the temple without telling a soul, and that you hope the political distractions in the capital will delay a serious inquiry while you attend to your many missteps these last few months."

The priest winced. His intensity of purpose remained evident, but he also looked disoriented, off-kilter.

The old woman continued, "But what I know most of all is that this boy, this Deer King, this *Dachahelu*…he will not die at your hands. Nor will he die at the hands of any other."

The priest stirred at this provocation. He unfurled his body to its full, towering height, looming above the woman like a turbulent thunderhead. "Move," he ordered.

The old woman ignored him. "I have a gift for you, ogre. Consider it an apology of sorts for tricking you with false offerings while keeping the real *Dachahelu* obscured from your sight." She looked up and pointed at Emmaline. "There stands the daughter of the Stoneman Brutus Rain. You've met before, I believe."

The priest followed the old woman's hand down the length of the dew oak with his black-hole eyes. He spotted Emmaline instantly. Emmaline felt the brutal chill of his recognition pass over her like a gust of winter wind.

When the priest spoke, his voice was empty and dark, a cavern of sound. "Does she have the other Saving Stone?"

"Of course not. I have the stone now. But she is yours to do with as you please. I advise you to take her as a gift and leave now, before you lose your life. But first, hand over your stone. You may leave with the girl, but you will not leave with the stone. If you're compelled to try otherwise, I'll make sure you don't leave at all."

In a flash, the tentative peace was broken. The priest reached for his dagger, but the old woman was faster: she raised her hand and touched the priest on his stationary arm, a cryptic word on her lips. At the sound of it, the priest's face turned ashen, and his knees buckled. For a moment he appeared incapacitated, but then he summoned a reserve of strength and pushed the old woman off him and to the ground.

The priest reached once more for this dagger, but this time an arrow sang out from the woods and lodged in his shoulder. Prala was standing at the tree line, bow in hand. The priest wheeled, saw Prala, and bellowed in frustration. Then the priest broke off the arrow near its shaft. He turned and cast his eyes at the hole in the tree for one last wanting moment. Jerking his eyes away, he cut his losses, and mounted the horse.

Once again, he charged toward Emmaline.

There was nowhere to run. Emmaline considered scaling the tree trunk and escaping to the other side, but the dew oak was too massive to quickly scale. She ran perhaps ten feet before the priest plucked her from the ground like a hawk snatching up a mouse. Using his good arm, the priest pinned her to his body and forced her to sit side saddle. She tested her strength against the priest's, with expected results.

Prala. Emmaline swiveled her head, searching for Prala at the tree line, fearful that he might launch an errant shot and kill her. As expected, he had notched another arrow, but he seemed disinclined to take the shot. Perhaps it was because they were out of range, but, whatever the reason, he simply stood there, watching them leave.

Emmaline's eyes went to the old woman. She was struggling back to her feet. She looked fragile, old, and, for the moment at least, bereft of power. But then the boy emerged from the dew oak, his eyes green cinders, and the old woman was made anew, hoisting herself upright and mouthing unheard invocations.

A swell of noise. The Massaporans came to violent life. A song of death in their throats. They tore after the Rugarder as one, ready to sacrifice themselves to bring the beast to its knees. But the priest and the horse were a seamless and powerful machine, and together they navigated the encroaching madness, forging a path with brute, efficient force: the horse blasted through what flesh and bone the priest couldn't circumvent, and soon the pursuing host was on their heels.

Within seconds they had cleared the village edge, and tore into the woods.

7

An endless blur of timber. The eastern sun an incandescent prisoner behind wooden bars. Promises of death backed by arrows thudding into bark. The persistent, percussive thump of hooves like scattershot hail on a tin roof, fast on flat ground, slower on uneven terrain, never letting up, ever heading south. Massaporan faces fading like apparitions in the trees. The priest keeping the horse on a road bed that vanished only to rematerialize time and again. Smaller, weaker horses, falling back. The priest's arm like an iron bolt shutting Emmaline in captivity. And then, when the imminent danger had faded, the unceasing sameness, hours of it, galloping cantering trotting, until they came upon a chattering brook and the priest slowed the horse first to a walk, and then to a stop.

The priest lowered Emmaline to the ground, not ungently. The blood in her body reclaimed abandoned outposts. Nearby, two grey squirrels played tag to a windy melody. Emmaline was thirsty, oh so thirsty, and the brook was enticing, so she walked over to it, stooped down, and took a drink. When she glanced up, the priest was kneeling beside her, filling his canteen. His pallor, she noticed, was considerably worse than before. He fixed her with dead eyes.

"The old woman took the stone you stole from me?"

She nodded. She was afraid of the priest, but having nearly died so many times these last few days had somewhat dulled her capacity for fear.

The priest sighed. He sunk into himself: it was like watching a speeded-up version of a mountain eroding. "That was her in the flesh," he said, looking away from Emmaline. "The Raven Queen. Now I know who I'm up against."

Emmaline said nothing. But she remembered the way the old woman had touched the priest, and how his face had turned ashen and his knees had buckled. It reminded her of when the old woman had touched her, and how, with a single word, she had brought death to Emmaline's doorstep.

She wondered if the priest was dying but didn't realize it.

The priest spent the next ten minutes tending to his shoulder. He made no effort to remove the arrowhead, instead pouring what looked to Emmaline to be whisky over the wound, and gently poking at the flesh surrounding it. Emmaline sat by the brook, taking the occasional drink from time to time. At last the priest put the flask of whisky away and stopped worrying at the wound. "Doshensa needs to have a look at this," he muttered to no one in particular. He turned to Emmaline. "I will not harm you, girl. You have done me a great wrong, but, because we are both children of the Bronze Titan, I will not take my revenge. I will return you to Mossbane, and hand you over to those who know you. And that will be the end of it."

"You killed my father," she said in response. The words weren't premeditated, but now that she had spoken, she knew that she wanted to see his reaction.

The priest looked Emmaline over as if he were seeing her for the first time. His eyes went dark again, caverns of inscrutable thought. "Did you see the boy when you were there?" he asked.

"Yes."

"And what did he look like to you?"

"He looked like a boy," she lied.

The priest frowned at her. "That boy will grow into a monster. He will kill any settler of Harrish descent by the thousands, if not the tens of thousands. Your father's job was to stop that boy being born. He failed in his task. Had he willingly turned over the Saving Stone, I would have spared his life. But he refused. So I took his life, and I took the stone, and I would damn well do it again."

"You failed too," she spat at him. "It's been over a year, and the boy is still alive."

He grabbed her by the wrist, lightning-quick, and jerked her in the same rag-doll fashion that he had jerked the sacrificial boy back in the village. Her bones rattled inside her body like a baby's toy. By the time her brain had sloshed back into place, the priest was gripping the index finger on her left hand. He snapped it in two like a raw carrot.

"I will break every bone in your body if you so much as speak a word about that boy once you are returned to Haven! Do you understand me? I will kill that boy! And as far as you are concerned, he is already dead!"

She heard his words, but the meaning was lost in a tsunami of pain. She might have screamed had she not lost her breath. She bit the inside of her mouth hard enough to draw blood, reflexively at first but then on purpose, the metallic taste gnawing at her senses until she could locate the flavor inside the shocking pain, and she focused on that, the taste of blood. Now that she was in control of herself again, she refused to scream or cry out. The blood swirled inside her mouth until the wave of pain crested and crashed, and then she laughed a jagged little laugh, knowing the top half of her finger was dangling and lost. It seemed funny to her. Then she spit some of the blood on the ground, and repeated herself to the priest once more.

"You failed too." And again. "You failed too."

The priest raised his hand as if he meant to strike her. But then the light of anger went out in his eyes and he looked like a lost boy, scared of the truth of what Emmaline had said. Without speaking, he grabbed Emmaline roughly, carried her over to the Rugarder, and mounted up.

They resumed their journey south.

In the cool of the evening, they approached a Massaporan village. A group of Massaporans hurried out to meet them. They wore wary but accommodating looks on their faces. Upon laying eyes on the priest and seeing his wound, they hurried Emmaline and the priest into the village proper.

Once inside the village, the priest and Emmaline dismounted in front of a wood and clay house. A middle-aged man adorned in large, pale-white feathers emerged. The man looked disconcerted when he saw the priest's wound.

"It's not our doing, I hope?" the man asked the priest in polished Harrish.

"It is," the priest replied.

The priest dismounted from the Rugarder, as did Emmaline. She noted that the ashen look in the priest's face had deepened. Behind the fleshy mask of his face she thought she could see the outline of his skull.

The man with the white feathers urged the priest to follow him into his home. The priest assented, but then, with a start, he remembered Emmaline. He turned to the nearby Massaporans and commanded that they keep close watch over her while he was gone. The man with the white feathers translated. Then the two of them disappeared inside.

Emmaline's four keepers, men all, stood around Emmaline in an awkward silence, their eyes flitting everywhere except her face. Except for one. He was a short fellow with inquisitive eyes, and when he exchanged glances with Emmaline, she thought he looked like a mouse, albeit one with bushy eyebrows. She assumed that he was weak because of his size, but then out of the blue he spoke to the others in a jarring, combative tenor, causing everyone to jump, Emmaline included. The others mumbled replies suggesting that they were uninterested in tangling with this strange, short man. He responded by barking at them a little more until they said nothing at all. Seemingly satisfied that he'd ensured their silence, the man pointed at Emmaline's broken finger, wanting a closer look.

She raised it in the air for him to see.

The others turned away. Mouse man, on the other hand, engaged in a series of clipped little head bobs that bespoke both enthusiastic concern and a ferocity of spirit. Then he put his index in the air and motioned for Emmaline to wait.

He returned minutes later holding two pieces of thinly shaved jorkwood, fine twine, and a leather-skin pouch. He held the pouch out for Emmaline, and then pantomimed that she should drink. She did. The clean, clear bite of corn alcohol scorched her throat. She took two swallows and tried to hand the pouch back. Mouse man spurned the pouch, motioned that she should drink more. Though her vision was already swimmy, she did as he suggested. Her throat burned again, but this time her body lightened. As she came back into herself, she thought she saw her soul flit away from her like a restless butterfly. She caught her soul with her right hand, and smiled at mouse man to celebrate the feat. He nodded as if he'd seen it too.

Or so she believed.

Mouse man motioned for her to give him her left hand, the one with the broken finger.

She complied.

When he set her broken bone back into place, the pain rang clear and light in her head like a morning bell. When the bell stopped ringing, she looked down at mouse man's handiwork. Her finger was a corpse inside the coffin of jorkwood, and mouse man was dabbing the jorkwood with a sticky, sap-like substance. Finished, he took the twine and tied it around Emmaline's finger while pressing it against the sticky substance on the jorkwood. Then he made clever little knots in the twine that looked like coils of snakes. When at last he was finished, Emmaline's finger, though badly pained, felt secure inside its splint.

"Thank you," she said. She felt that she needed to offer him something more than her appreciation. But the only gift she could think to offer was her name, so she offered him that. "Emmaline," she said, pointing at herself.

He nodded to indicate that he understood. Then he stuck his own finger at his chest.

"Twichi," he offered in turn.

After setting Emmaline's finger, Twichi insisted that she follow him home. The other men charged with watching over Emmaline took umbrage when Twichi led her away, but he flicked his wrist at them and made sucking noises with his teeth until they stopped.

Twichi lived in a small log house near the village edge with his wife and two small children. His abode had a symmetry and sturdiness that put the others Massaporan houses to shame. Emmaline had a strong suspicion that he had constructed it himself.

After meeting Twichi's wife and children—the wife had the look and mannerisms of an industrious beaver, while the kids, who appeared to be between two and four years of age, seemed possessed of an inexhaustible energy—the first thing Emmaline noticed was the triangular symbol that she had seen in the Deer King's village, carved into the log that hung over Twichi's front door. Drifting in a pleasant corn alcohol haze, she walked over and touched the symbol, remembering too late what had happened the last time a Massaporan saw her affect the mysterious mark. She flinched and withdrew her hand upon realizing what she was doing, but, when she turned to see Twichi's reaction, he was not only unbothered, he appeared to encourage her: he nodded his head approvingly and, between fits of chewing on the shoot of an unknown plant, said *"Weesh, Dachahelu, weesh, weesh."*

She wished they spoke a common language so that she might unburden herself of a few questions. She started to say something in Harrish but she lost her words in the overripe, late-evening sky. The familial atmosphere was affecting her: she realized in an inebriated epiphany that she wanted nothing so much as she wanted to belong. For an instant, her thoughts turned melancholic as she reminisced on Oostri, Clay, and Seywa, and the way that Shayo had betrayed her. In short order her father and brother appeared, their faces flashing perfectly clear for a moment, only to be lost again, and once more become blurred, smudgy memories. Yet another memory rose from the mists. The boy. The Deer King. He stared up at her with large, wanting eyes, a perfect, pristine memory. In that instant she felt a connection to him like an electric shock thrumming the core of her being.

She was still thinking of the boy when the priest and the man with the white feathers approached. They would have caught her unaware had Twichi not stood up and walked over to meet them. The priest's shoulder was dressed in white bandages, doubly covered by billowing vestments. He looked marginally better than before, but his eyes were still far-off, and his face remained a pallid recess. Emmaline stared at him. He did not stare back.

Twichi and the man with the white feathers exchanged a series of hushed inflections. Even in a lower register Emmaline detected Twichi's matter-of-fact, confrontational lilt. The man with the white feathers responded tit for tat. When it was over, the man with the white feathers turned and addressed Emmaline in Harrish.

"You will stay here with my nephew and his family tonight. In the morning we will escort the priest across the border to Mossbane. You will go with him."

The man with the white feathers didn't wait for a response. Guiding the priest by the shoulder, the two of them turned to go.

Twichi awoke Emmaline in the cool dark of the morning, in the hour before the birds sing awake the sun. He made her corn cakes and potatoes over a fresh fire, then urged her to quickly eat. He stared intently at her while she ate. It seemed to Emmaline that he had something he wanted to say, only the language barrier was getting in the way.

She finished eating minutes before sunrise. Daylight brought with it the priest and the man with the white feathers atop the Rugarder and a dapple grey, respectively, ready to move south.

Seeing the men arrive, Emmaline turned to say goodbye to Twichi, but he was already walking away. The mystery of his kindness continued to baffle her, but there was no time at the present to unravel it.

The man with the white feathers offered Emmaline his arm. When she grabbed it, he swung her onto the horse. She had assumed that she would ride with the priest, but it appeared the man with the white feathers wanted to spare the priest the labor of riding tandem.

At first the trip resembled her flight with the priest from the day before, an endless parade of blood elms, dew oaks, and supple jorkwoods, but after a couple of hours the forest welcomed less imposing types of timber, white poplars and snow birch and a multitude of saplings. There was a change in the air as well: earthy zephyrs replaced the sweetly crisp winds of Wolfresh. The wind batted familiarly at Emmaline's face. After more than a year away, she was almost home.

She glanced ahead at the priest. He was drawn up around himself like a cave. She thought again of the old woman's touch, and wondered if the priest was being slowly drained of his life force by a magic that would kill him once he crossed the Havenese border.

I hope so, she thought. *He deserves to die.*

They entered the outlying areas of Mossbane mid-afternoon. The priest and the man with the white feathers grew more alert, stacking their spines in the saddle. Emmaline hadn't seen the priest's face the entire ride, so she couldn't tell if he was faring better or worse than before. They rode past a handful of outlying houses without being noticed, but then, when they were perhaps a quarter mile from the town proper, a farmer saw them and stole ahead.

By the time they entered Mossbane, a crowd had gathered along the main thoroughfare. Everywhere Emmaline looked, familiar faces filled in the gaps, rekindling flames of memory in Emmaline's mind. Every countenance wore an expression of bewilderment. Emmaline's name rang out. Emmaline searched the crowd and saw Regina Houghton among the assembled, calling for her. Emmaline gave an awkward little wave in return, not knowing what else to do.

The man with the white feathers brought his horse to a stop, as did the priest. To Emmaline's surprise, the man with the white feathers spoke.

"I am Doshensa, healer and one of the seven *Koeceti* of the Wolfresh nation. As such I am authorized to travel outside of Wolfresh and speak on behalf of my people, as is stipulated in the *Wolfresh-Potter Accord*. Kern, great priest of the Bronze Titan, came to me in search of treatment for a wound that he had suffered at the hands of a renegade group of Massaporans known to worship *Dachahelu*, more commonly known in the Harrish tongue as the Deer King. I now return him safely to a land beyond the borders of Wolfresh, and into the arms of a people who keep the faith of the one true god, the Bronze Titan."

The one true god? Emmaline remembered Twichi proudly showing her the symbol of the Deer King carved into the front of his house. Were there Massaporans who worshipped the

Bronze Titan as well? Or was this all a ruse for the citizens of Mossbane's benefit?

Doshensa's horse stepped backwards, and flipped its restless tail. Doshensa continued, "To show that no terms of the *Wolfresh-Potter Accord* have been violated, I ask the priest to attest that he remains in possession of a Saving Stone."

Without saying a word, the priest reached into a hidden pocket in his vestments and brought out the Saving Stone. Emmaline caught a glimpse of his face in profile: he looked damaged, like an egg with a crack. He flashed the stone at the crowd with a look of contempt. Then he hid it away again.

Doshensa nodded solemnly as if this had been a moment of great import. Satisfied, he turned and grabbed Emmaline around the waist, helping her dismount. Once she was off, Doshensa's dapple grey began pacing this way and that. It was difficult to tell if the horse was behaving at Doshensa's urging or by its own volition. "Now I take my leave," Doshensa said. "See that the priest is cared for."

Doshensa turned his horse to go, but before he could, a voice rang out from the crowd.

"Is the Deer King dead?"

An uneasy quiet descended, like the sound of carrion birds lighting on a carcass. Doshensa played his response masterfully, turning to the priest, and, in doing so, directing the attention of the crowd toward the priest as well. Emmaline's gaze followed everyone else's.

The priest hatched a disturbing, crooked smile. The many lines on his face looked like the scrawled lines of a poem written by death.

"Yes," he lied.

8

The priest rode on to The Last Traveler, Mossbane's only inn. Doshensa turned the dapple grey around and left. Emmaline stood in the middle of the street, watching them go.

Regina Houghton approached, trailed by her husband, Dillon. "Let's get you home before the questions start," Regina said, pulling Emmaline away from the encroaching crowd. Much like a year earlier when she had followed Oostri's clan, Emmaline complied for lack of a better option.

They walked the two-mile trek out to the Houghtons' in silence. Emmaline sensed that the Houghtons had a million questions but wanted to give Emmaline space. A quarter mile away from the Houghtons' home, Emmaline caught a glimpse of her childhood cabin through a tangle of trees. Through the broken vista, the cabin looked like a fragmented dream.

The Houghtons served rabbit for supper, the same garlicky concoction as the last time she had been there. The sensory memory of the last time both her brother and father had been alive triggered silent tears. Regina thought the tears were an invitation to pry, but, when Emmaline met her questions with the same silence that had occasioned her crying, the queries drifted away like wisps of smoke. When supper was finished, Dillon Houghton looked at Emmaline and said, "You've got the rest of your days to figure out what you want to say. There's no rush."

Dillon's words played in Emmaline's head later that night as she lay in bed, trying to drift off to sleep. *The rest of your days.* After all that she'd been through, and after all that she'd seen, the thought that her part in the incipient drama of the Deer King's life was effectively over, and that she would have the rest of her life to make sense of it, galled. She, whose father had been a Stoneman. She, who had bested the great priest of the Bronze Titan and stolen a Saving Stone. She, who had parleyed with the Raven Queen. She, who had called the Deer King by his true name and soothed his troubled soul. She, whose last name was Rain. *No,* she thought, *I will not be cast out of the story of my life.*

But then what role would she play? She sat up in bed. Tried to clear her head. But the Houghtons' cabin was too stifling for rational thought. She climbed out of bed and crept past the Houghtons, outside the cabin into the Havenese night.

The night was alive with weather. Up above, a cavalry of luminescent clouds stormed across a field of stars, stirred to action by the trumpeting of winds. Somewhere far off, the sky growled, though whether it was thunder or moaning winds, it was impossible to say. Emmaline braced herself against the swirling gusts, relishing their wild caresses. They cleared her mind with the sudden force of a blunt truth. *I do have a role to play. But I don't yet have the knowledge to play my role well.* She needed to know more about the Deer King. She needed to know more about the history of her people and the history of the Massaporans. And then, once she had that knowledge, she could decide for herself if the Deer King was a deity that deserved to be saved, or deserved to be killed.

She began the walk back to Mossbane. And as she walked, she formed a plan. If she truly wanted to play a part in the paramount story of her life, she needed power. Without power she was simply the orphaned daughter of a Stoneman, destined to live out her life as little more than a local curiosity, the object of scorn and pity. But with power she might forge her own destiny, yoke her own story once more to those forces which would, for better or worse, shape her life.

Everything became clear. She knew exactly what she was going to do. It was a forty-minute, two-mile trek to The Last Traveler, Mossbane's only inn. The priest was inside. Sleeping, possibly dying.

And on the priest was the Saving Stone.

By the time Emmaline reached Mossbane, the heavens had opened. The frontier city's buildings, which resembled more a sprawling collection of structures rather than a uniform whole, had hunkered into themselves for the storm, every candle snuffed out and every window closed shut. The single exception was The Last Traveler. Edgar Broggs, the proprietor, kept a single candle lit to signify vacancies. Through the blinding squall, Emmaline could just make it out in the window.

She was soaked when she arrived: her buckskin dress was dark with water, and her very bones felt soft and swollen from the rain, like puffy bread. Her first instinct was to get out of the rain, but she forced herself to take the lay of the land first. She looked for a place to hide. She settled on a willow tree opposite the inn. The tree's slender leaves cascaded from the heights like a bounty of slicked hair. Underneath, Emmaline hid behind one of the longer flows, and from there spied on the inn.

Nothing appeared amiss. Every window save the front was dark, and, to the best that Emmaline could tell, no shadows roamed the interior. While she watched, the rain began to taper into thinner and thinner sheets, until at last the droplets were once again distinguishable from one another. Calling on a memory at least two years old, Emmaline tried her best to visualize the inside of the inn. The foyer inside the front door spilled into a large common room. To the left was the kitchen.

Tucked behind the kitchen and located on the backside of the house was Edgar and Anne Broggs's bedroom. Turning right past the foyer led to a straight staircase, and past the staircase were three bedrooms. Up the stairs were six additional bedrooms, three on each side of the bannister.

The priest could be in any one of them.

Resolved, Emmaline marched out of her hiding place and crossed over to the inn. Halfway there, a scything moon slashed open the belly of a dark cloud, exposing her to the world. Instinctively, she picked up the pace. As she stepped onto the inn's white wooden porch, she couldn't help but worry that she had been seen.

Reaching the doorstep, she tested the knob. As expected, there was no barrier to entry. Timing her movements to the patter of the rain, Emmaline eased inside. Turned right. The wooden floors threatened a greeting with every step, but Emmaline's footsteps were feathers, making the floor's salutations little more than sighs. Passing the staircase, she got her first glimpse of the downstairs bedrooms. Two of the rooms had open doors like wanting mouths. Only one door—the middle bedroom in the group—was closed.

Before the enormity and the dangerousness of what she was attempting could stop her, Emmaline approached the closed door and opened it. Inside, a topography of swells covered the bed. *It's him,* she thought. She looked for living land, a respiratory rise and fall. After a moment she spotted it: the plateau of the priest's chest fluttered like a rippling lake, suggesting the possibility of life. Undeterred by the possibility that he might still be alive, she approached the head of the bed, and positioned herself for a look at his face.

The priest's eyes shot open and his hand sprang to life, grabbing her by the left wrist.

She didn't scream. Not when she saw his empty, soot-black eyes and not when his familiar grip threatened to break another bone. She stared back at him, fearless. She had stared into a god's eyes and seen the horror of the ages—why would she be scared of a dying man's empty and vacant stare? In a moment she knew that she was right: the priest's grip weakened and his stare collapsed back into itself like quicksand. She thought he was dying at that very moment, but then he drew a breath, and she realized that he was transferring what little remaining energy he had left to his voice.

"The…(gasp)…Raven…(gasp)…Queen.
She's…(gasp)…killed me."

He found her with his eyes. His head a withered stalk. She wasn't sure, but it appeared as if he recognized her.

He spoke again, his voice desperate and yearning. "Remember…(gasp)…what…I…(gasp)…told…you.   The boy…(gasp)…must die."

She refused to nod. She thought herself an angel of death, come to visit the priest at the appointed hour. She wasn't here to take orders. She was here to take the stone.

The priest groaned, losing eye contact. She didn't hesitate. She patted him down, searching for the stone, the jorkwood cast on her left index finger scratching the sheets. The priest was still dressed in his vestments—he appeared to have come to his room and gone directly to bed—so that when she patted his ribcage, she found the stone hidden in an interior pocket, presumably the same pocket from which she had stolen the other stone a year prior. The weight of the stone surprised her: it was almost twice as heavy as the one the Raven Queen now possessed.

Her instincts stung her like a scorpion. *Leave now.* She turned to go, but from somewhere in the house she heard the creak of trodden floorboards, and, to her surprise, not one but two sets of footsteps. She froze long enough to confirm her fears. Not knowing what part of the house the footsteps were coming from, she took a risk and left the priest's room, closing the door quietly behind her before slipping into the next room further down the hall. She moved along the room's wall until she was out of sight of the hallway, and then she went as still as a rock, her only movement the slight tremble of her breathing.

She waited and listened. After a moment she heard the hushed whispers of Edgar Broggs and his wife, Anne.

"No more arguing. You check on him, Edgar. I know a sick man when I see one."

"It won't go over well if I wake the priest from his sleep, my dear. Guests don't take kindly to being rustled awake in the dead of night."

"You'll do it if needs be. I know he told you not to send for the doctor, but he's a stubborn sort, the sort that would rather die than admit he's dying. I'll apologize if I'm wrong. But if he's on death's doorstep, you'll go next door and bring Doc Pritchard back with you."

They reached the priest's room, and the whispering stopped. The door opened and someone entered the priest's room. Emmaline listened with a desperate intensity, but for the next minute or two she heard nothing. Then, once more, the married couple resumed whispering.

"He *is* fading, Anne. Short of breath and he looks like a fresh corpse. I'm sorry... I should have heeded your advice. Go in and keep a watch on him. It won't take me a minute to rouse Doc Pritchard. I'll be back shortly."

Edgar's footsteps scuttled away. Anne trod softly into the priest's room. Once again the inn went quiet.

The silence expanded like a bubble until it was popped by the soft hush of Anne's nervous singing. Under cover of the melody, Emmaline moved closer to the door. Pricked her ears. She didn't recognize the song at first, but then it came to her. *Shores upon Shores*. The song was a melancholic hymn sung in the temple of the Bronze Titan, a song that had originated during the time of The Great Torquec War. A fitting tune for a deathbed. Beneath the melody, Emmaline thought she could hear the priest's death rattle.

Now that she was closer to the door, Emmaline verified what she had suspected: the door to the priest's room remained open, which meant there was no way for her to escape without risking being seen. She weighed her options. She could run and risk exposing herself, or she could wait in the hopes that everyone would eventually leave and she'd have a clear path for an escape. With Edgar and Doc Pritchard due to return, and with the priest on the verge of death, she knew that there was only one real option.

She had to leave now.

She had scarcely taken her first step when she heard the creak of a floorboard. It was a soft creak, befitting either a cat or an intruder. She listened for the sound again. Her eyes rather than her ears were rewarded: a shadow appeared in the hallway, lithe and clever, contorting itself in such a way that it stayed out of sight of the priest's doorway, although Emmaline could see it from her vantage point. The shadow crept forward inch by inch, stalking the room. Emmaline, pinned against the wall, worried that the person who belonged to the shadow would see her if they continued advancing, but then, with a movement so quick it scarce seemed to have happened, a man appeared in the doorway of the priest's room and entered, failing to notice Emmaline at all.

Emmaline didn't have to wait long to discover the intruder's intent. Anne Broggs made two sounds: the first a befuddled coo that brought the singing to an end, and the second a scream that died in its infancy. Fear momentarily paralyzed Emmaline: she didn't know whether to run or to hide. But then the muscle memory of survival kicked in, and she retreated, sliding back along the wall away from the door.

Bedlam erupted at the sound of Anne's scream. Upstairs, a guest opened their door and cried out, "Is everything all right?"

Then a different, distant door opened, followed by the sound of footsteps. Edgar Broggs, newly returned, shouted, "What's the matter?" to the upstairs guest, his voice full of false bravado. "There was a scream…" came the reply, but the guest's response was interrupted by the shadow come to life, a Massaporan man stepping into the hallway looking wild and flustered. The man had a long face that registered in Emmaline's subconscious a split second before she processed who it was. Prala. Prala, sensing her presence, turned and stuck his head in the room. When he saw her, understanding dawned on his face. He had come to steal the stone from the priest, but she had beat him to it, and now there was nothing he could do.

Behind Prala came a rumble of footsteps. He turned to face his fate.

When Edgar and Doc Pritchard crashed into Prala, it was like a colliding of planets. The three men fell across the face of the door, landing with a violent *thump*. A struggle ensued: Edgar grunted and Doc Pritchard swore and Prala made no sound at all. Footsteps clump-clumped down the stairs. The guest—a scrappy-looking pilgrim—flashed across the doorway and joined in the assault. Emmaline knew without a doubt who the winners would be.

Now.

She was out the doorway in an instant. The Saving Stone clenched in her right hand, the men a peripheral blur. They shouted *Stop!* and other words that Emmaline couldn't decipher, but the business with Prala was too intensive to spare the able-bodied, so no one followed. She burst out the front door and into a night scrubbed fresh by the rain.

She ran west, away from civilization. Into the woods. The trees and the clouds and the night sky cloaked her in a hardy blackness. Her worry that she was being followed dissipated with each passing second. She dodged trees with an effortless grace, her feet guiding her back to the Houghtons. Soon she was on the same dirt road that she had traversed many times in her youth, the uneasy quiet of the woods all around her.

She slowed to a walk. Brought her breathing back under control. The world righted and the realization of what she had done washed over her. She stopped and brought the stone to eye level. Her personal conduit to the Deer King. The stone weighed heavy in her hand like original sin. But she felt no guilt. None at all.

She looked deep into the stone's blue-grey face.

"*Dachahelu*," she whispered.

9

She slipped back into the Houghtons' cabin in the small hours of the morning. Dillon awoke when she returned, groggy but conscious enough to note her return. "Where did you go?" he asked.

"Outhouse," Emmaline whispered in reply. Dillon nodded and dozed back off to sleep.

Regina Houghton shook Emmaline awake a few hours later. The sun was a newborn in the sky. There was a frenzied look in Regina's eyes. "Boy from town brought news this morning," she said to Emmaline. "Your priest and the innkeeper's wife are dead. Murdered. Plus, the Saving Stone is missing. Word has it they've captured a native. He's to hang later in the day."

Emmaline said nothing. Regina noticed Emmaline's buckskin dress, the way it lay damp against her skin. Her face screwed up in confusion, but only for a moment; she quickly willed her disconcertion away, a tranquil expression taking its place. "This heathen's dress won't do. We're going into town for the hanging. You'll wear my extra petticoat and gown."

The petticoat and gown felt like a layer of dead snake skin, obscuring Emmaline's true self. But when they arrived in Mossbane later that day, Emmaline was glad for the camouflage: Mossbane was teeming with humanity, the news of Prala's impending execution having traveled far and fast. Executions in Mossbane being infrequent, there had been no time to construct a gallows, but a stunted dew oak—a rarity this far south—had been appropriated for the occasion, a noose hanging from its branches. Scores upon scores of people loitered around the tree, staking out a prime vantage point from which to view the proceedings. Emmaline knew that were she wearing the buckskin dress, she would have drawn an excessive amount of attention, but in the petticoat and gown, only those close enough to confirm her identity showed interest, cupping their hands over their mouths and speculating about the past year of her life to their hearts' content.

They brought Prala out at noon sharp. The damage done to him by Doc Pritchard and the others made his lengthy face look even longer: Prala's countenance was smeared with bruises to the degree that he resembled a piece of fruit gone to rot, his skin oozing purple, blue, and black. But he held his head high as the sheriff—a forty-year-old man named Henry Malls—led him to the dew oak. A procession of Prala's captors trailed in the sheriff's wake: stocky, white-chinned Edgar Broggs; broad-shouldered, bald-headed Doc Pritchard; and the inn's guest, a wiry man with a moustache that reminded Emmaline of her brother.

The five men stood and faced the crowd. Apparently there were matters of business to attend to before the hanging could commence.

Sheriff Malls spoke first. "This native stands accused of entering The Last Traveler last night and murdering both Anne Broggs and Kern, a high priest of the Bronze Titan. Edgar, Doc Pritchard and...What's your name again, son?"

The wiry traveler responded with a scratchy voice, "Reed Hall, sir."

"...and Reed Hall all attest to the fact. As this native is not one of the seven *Koeceti*, he is also guilty of trespassing on

Havenese territory. As such, I condemn this man to death by hanging, by the power vested in me by the Havenese Territorial Legislature. But first, there's another matter to address."

The sheriff stepped back, and Edgar stepped forward. The innkeeper's eyes were wet with tears, and his face was red with emotion. He looked like someone was strangling his happiness. It took a great effort for him to speak.

"Like the sheriff said, this savage took my Anne from me last night. Not only that, he killed the priest..."

"I did not kill the priest," Prala interrupted.

Gasps populated the crowd, followed by a low murmuring. The crowd was shocked to hear Prala speak: his bruises made him appear inhuman, which Emmaline thought doubled the effect of his voice. Reed Hall, piqued by the disruption, lashed out.

"The savage is a liar!" he shouted to the assembled. With his fervor and his moustache, he looked both righteous and demonic. "Yes, the priest died after we apprehended the heathen, but, make no mistake, it was the Massaporan's evil that did it! I heard him snap the innkeeper's wife's neck with my own two ears. Then, when we went to check on the priest once we had captured the savage, the priest was on death's doorstep. And this only moments after the Massaporan had left the priest's room. Now every good soul of Harrish descent knows the black magic these heathens are capable of. So don't be fooled by this trickster's words. He killed the priest. Have no doubts about it!"

A chorus of "huzzahs!" resounded. There were plenty in the crowd who had seen the priest's sickly pallor yesterday, but Reed's detailing of the case was enough to sway the already-biased citizenry. Doc Pritchard and Edgar, who knew otherwise, said nothing. For his part, Prala made no further objections: Emmaline wondered if Reed had conveyed the gist of what he wanted heard.

Edgar continued. "Thank you, sir," he said, nodding at Reed. "I will have justice for my wife's death shortly. But the people of Mossbane should know that this savage was not working alone last night. A different Massaporan—a woman, we think—stole out of the inn while we were subduing my wife's murderer. We saw her run off, but she had too much of a head start to catch her. When we searched the priest after he died, we were unable to find the Saving Stone. We believe the Massaporan woman took it north."

Another round of murmurings. Emmaline heard snippets of the chatter. 'They will die for it, they will. The lot of them. That's the Accord broken. We won't be safe now until all of Wolfresh is razed.' She swiveled her head and saw death on every tongue. *They mistook me for a Massaporan,* she thought. *Now they have an excuse to invade.* Her heart began to beat the way it had in Wolfresh when she thought she was going to die. She reached down and brushed her hand against the Saving Stone, hidden in a pocket beneath her petticoat. In a moment's madness she considered pulling the stone from the pocket and showing it to the townspeople. She would explain that the Accord was not broken, that the hounds of death need not be unleashed. But the moment passed and the vengeful barking carried on.

The sheriff stepped forward again. He was chip-toothed and mousy-haired, which made him hard to take seriously, but he also knew how to muster a fire in his voice. He did so now. "I asked Edgar to speak so that you'd hear it straight from the source. Early this morning, I sent word to both the Havenese Legislature and the capital of Olgard to let them know that the priest was dead and the Saving Stone was missing. They'll likely send out an investigative commission. And maybe, if they're not too distracted by the mess going on in Brine, an army. Regardless, a change is coming on the winds. Between now and then we had best get prepared. I was a boy the last time the heathens came south. Those of us who were alive will never forget the hell they brought with them. This time we'll greet them with fire and blood."

The people responded with hard, mirthless cheers. The current of their fervor carried Prala up a horse-drawn cart, the sheriff leading from behind. Together, the two men rode until the cart was beneath the tree. Emmaline watched as the sheriff slipped the noose over Prala's neck. Prala's eyes flashed opened and closed. A word materialized on his tongue, the same four syllables over and over. Although she couldn't hear him, Emmaline knew what he was saying. She unconsciously mouthed the word back at him.

Dachahelu.

The sheriff jumped off the cart. An expectant silence fell over the crowd. Prala's mumblings suddenly became audible, a secret on the wind. The man leading the horse started to urge the colt forward, but then a question rang out from the crowd.

"What are you saying, savage? Let us hear your last words!"

Prala stopped speaking. His eyes opened. His gaze wandered over the crowd, empty and serene, lighting upon one group of people and then another like a fickle bird deciding upon a branch. Then, to Emmaline's shock, his gaze fell upon her. She was standing near thirty yards away in a congested throng, so it was impossible for the others to know who he was looking at, but she had no doubt where his stare was directed. He gave her a small smile. A smile like a thick pane of glass; like a dull knife; like a cold and unknowable stone. He held her with it until her heart turned cold. Then his gaze drifted off into the heavens.

"The Dachahelu will kill you all," he said simply to the crowd. When they started to scream at him, he closed his eyes once more, and awaited his fate.

The horse started its death march. Prala's feet shuffled along the bottom of the cart, heading toward the precipice. Knowing what was coming, Emmaline turned and walked away from the now frothing crowd.

The Saving Stone bounced heavy on her thigh as she went.

AUTHOR'S NOTE

If you enjoyed the book and would like to see the series grow, please consider reviewing THE DEER KING over at Amazon and Goodreads. Be sure to visit benspencerwrites.com for updates on new releases in the series. Thank you!

I'm writing to you in January of 2018, a couple of weeks before the first novella in THE DEER KING series is finished. Thank you for taking the time to read the inaugural story. I hope that what you've just experienced will inspire you to travel a little longer on this journey with me, and, if the trip continues to hold your interest, perhaps remain my traveling companion until the end of the series.

I've had the idea for THE DEER KING series for a couple of years now. Ideas, as they say, are a dime a dozen, but, as time passed, THE DEER KING demanded my attention in a way that few of my other writing projects have, until, like a teacher unable to ignore the earnest student with a raised hand, I called it to the forefront. Why? I've long been fascinated with the colonial period, and I thought that creating a fantasy world that explored the dynamics between the indigenous peoples and the settlers offered a bevy of possibilities. Without explaining away the process, I believed that adding a few twists to the conceit might reframe our own perceptions of the Age of Colonialism in a compelling way. Although this particular story was told from Emmaline's point of view, I plan to paint a broader landscape as time goes on by exploring similar themes from different viewpoints. Emmaline will remain a central figure throughout—don't worry, there are more tales to come from her POV—but the story of the Massaporan people is vital to the heart of the series, and I want to create characters who will do the Massaporans' viewpoint justice.

One of the reasons I'm most excited about the series is that I believe that writing the series in novella form will make it remain urgent in a way that trilogies sometimes do not. I'm a slow (though consistent) writer, so writing novellas will allow me to put out work every four to six months. I know many fantasy readers enjoy devouring a trilogy in one extended setting, but, if you're like me, the idea of checking in with a novella every few months sounds like a fascinating way to grow with a series. There may be a few deviations along the way—I enjoy non-linear timelines, and I make no promises that every story will further the plot of the previous one—but, as is clear from Story One, the series is heading toward a day when the fate of the present Deer King will ultimately be determined.

Once again, thank you for reading the first story. I'm planning on releasing the first two or three novellas together, so hopefully you have the next novella queued up and ready to go. If you're nervous about missing future releases of THE DEER KING series, please visit my website at benspencerwrites.com and sign up to follow the blog. You'll then receive an email every time I update my website. I promise to update my website every time I release a new novella. Also, be sure to check out the website for interesting tidbits about The Deer King series, as well as links to some of my other works, if you're so inclined.

Until next time…